Suffer the Flesh

Anthologies by Monica J. O'Rourke

Black October Magazine (senior editor)
Decadence
Dreaming of Angels (co-edited with Gord Rollo)
No Quarter (co-edited)
Random Acts of Weirdness (co-edited with Brian Knight)
Royal Aspirations III
Space & Time (assistant editor)

Suffer the Flesh

Monica J. O'Rourke

PRIME O
Canton, Ohio

For Adrienne Scott, friend and mentor, who showed me how to reinvent myself.

Special thanks to Teri Jacobs, Brian Knight, Don Nault, Jack Fisher, Mark West, and Rob Swartwood for countless hours reading and offering valuable advice and friendship; Dr. Oscar Rodriguez for his insight and medical expertise; Sean Wallace for his help above and beyond the usual; and my family, for their love and support.

SUFFER THE FLESH

Published in the United States by **prime**
P.O. Box 36503, Canton, OH 44735
www.primebooks.net

ISBN:1-894815-35-1

Oh! Dreadful is the check—intense the agony—
When the ear begins to hear, and the eye begins to see;
When the pulse begins to throb, The brain to think again; the soul to feel the
flesh, and the flesh to feel the chain

Emily Bronte

Chapter 1

I can help you.

Those had been the words, words that started it all, words that changed Zoey's life.

She turned the corner of Fourteenth Street at Union Square, bumped into a vendor hawking honey-roasted nuts, watched a skinny Jimmy Walker lookalike sell fake Rolex watches out of a leather briefcase worth more than the items he was trying to unload. Mobs of downtown Manhattan commuters rushed past her into oblivion. She ducked into a bookstore on Seventeenth Street.

"I can help you."

Clutching a book to her chest she glanced at the woman standing beside her. Zoey knelt before the endless volumes of dieting self-help on the Barnes and Noble shelves. "Excuse me?"

The woman knelt beside Zoey and flipped her long blonde hair over one shoulder. "I can help."

Zoey blinked. "I think you've confused me with someone else. I didn't ask for help."

"But you want it, don't you?"

"What?" Zoey stood, her knees popping. She scratched an itch on her eyebrow and shifted the books from one hand to the other.

The woman followed her up from the crouch. "Hey, look, it's no biggie. It's just . . . well, I've been there. I know what it's like. I know how to fix it."

Zoey didn't know what the odd woman was talking about, only knew that it wasn't the most uncommon thing to have a few unstable people approach you when you lived in New York City. Even in Barnes and Noble. Even crazies enjoyed a good read.

Shrugged and laughed nervously and moved slowly away from Powter and Atkins and sidled toward New Age.

"My name's Mel. As in Melody. Would you stop moving away for just a minute?"

Zoey stopped. Trailed a finger along the shelf as if inspecting for dust. Then she saw it coming. The expression on Mel's face, the way she cocked her head and pursed her lips and squinted her eyes. That look of judgment. Zoey knew what was next—the commentary. The advice. A few hundred cliches. Zoey often had retorts for them, but mostly not. Most of the time it wasn't worth it, and retorts rarely had the desired impact.

Zoey sighed, crossed her arms over her chest. "What is it?"

"I used to be your size."

Knew it. "What are you selling? Weight Watchers? Jennie Craig? NutriSystem?"

"No."

Zoey waited for Mel to continue. Felt her cheeks flush with embarrassment, and anger toward her own reaction. Why was it that she felt the need to accept other people's views of her?

"It's not a diet."

"Pills then. Supplements?" She'd heard it all. Metabolism boosts, speed, all-protein diets, all liquids, all fruit, count calories, count fat grams, exercise till you drop. There was nothing new out there.

"Will you let me finish?"

Again, her cheeks flushed, reduced to this by a total stranger.

"I didn't mean to embarrass you. But you'd never guess, because it's not a diet or pills, nothing like that. It's . . . well, it's more of a regimen."

"What, a fat camp?" Zoey laughed. "If you're trying to sell me something, you're not very good at it."

Mel smiled sadly. "It's just . . . See, this isn't . . ." She pulled at her lip, twisted the corner. "I shouldn't even be telling you this. There are recruitment requirements."

"Recruitment? What is it, boot camp? Is this for the military?"

Mel shook her head.

Now Zoey was intrigued. She noticed how attractive Mel was, how thin, and she felt a twinge of jealousy as she often did when seeing a thin, beautiful woman.

"Are you interested?" Mel asked.

In what? She didn't know any more now than a few minutes ago. "What's the cost?"

"No cost. Are you married?"

"Married? No—why?" Zoey tilted her head.

"What's your name, anyway?"

"Zoey."

"Kids, Zoey? Pets? Serious relationship?"

"No to all of the above. But—"

"You're a perfect candidate. No commitments."

"For what?" She swallowed, not sure why she suddenly felt apprehensive. A no-cost plan that didn't include dieting. But now she was getting the third degree from Mel, this unusual woman she'd met only minutes before. What was there not to be wary of?

It reminded her of a sales pitch she'd received a year earlier, a company trying to convince her they were the wave of the future in telecommunications and that she should invest huge sums of money and become a seller. The truth was, everything had a catch. A price.

"So this is free? And I'll lose weight?"

"Absolutely. I used to be a size twenty, and now I'm a six."

"What's the catch?"

"Look—I'm not supposed to say anything else. They already know you're interested—"

"They?"

"—So my part of this is over. Good luck, Zoey." Mel turned away and headed toward the escalator. Glanced back over her shoulder as she descended. "Please don't hate me . . . "

Mel's parting words sat like a rock in the pit of Zoey's stomach.

Reading and book buying were suddenly of no interest. This was too bizarre. She needed chocolate.

Zoey headed uptown, found a Baskin and Robbins and ordered a rocky road sundae. Her attempts at death by chocolate were never fatal.

Wiped the corner of her mouth with the back of her hand because she'd forgotten the napkins. Mel's words ran through her head, and little of it made sense; she'd been so cryptic.

Who were *they*? And when were they going to contact her? How could they?

Headed west, toward the subway, toward the N train that would bring her home to Queens. Several blocks from her destination she was approached by an aggressive homeless man, asking for spare change.

She tried to ignore him, to maneuver around him, but he kept blocking her. She moved toward the curb but he was faster, seemed to anticipate her moves. He smelled like urine and sweat, his hands crusted with grime.

Looked around, searched for help, a waste of time in a city that wasn't known as the City of Brotherly Love. Passers-by inspected the sidewalk as they rushed past, giving wide berth to the lunatic confronting her.

"C'mon, girlie, cost ya'a quawta ta pass." He grinned, surprisingly white teeth, somehow more startling. There was something disturbing in his smile, something she couldn't determine in those fleeting moments.

"You got too much food in ya', girlie."

In spite of her fear, in spite of the dread, embarrassment spread on her cheeks like a disease. To reference her weight was the secret weapon. Zoey was ready to wave the white flag, to empty the contents of her wallet into his filthy, diseased hands just to shut him up. To detract attention away from her, from her size. He was a dirty fighter and she was defenseless against him.

"What's going on here?" Police officer. Zoey's heart sank. Had he heard the lunatic's last remarks? "You okay, miss? He hurt you?"

The homeless man was being cuffed and led into an unmarked police car. She hadn't even noticed them approach.

"Come on," he said. "We'll give you a ride home."

"It's okay, I live in Queens. I can take the train."

He smiled, his lingering gaze making her uncomfortable. His eyes roamed her thighs, hips, stomach, chest, face. As if sizing her up. She couldn't tell if that was disgust in his eyes. There were men out there who were attracted to large women, but she had yet to find one.

"Not a problem," he said, his brown eyes droopy. He took off and replaced his cap, revealing a severely receding hairline. "It's S.O.P." He waved his arm toward the unmarked car, the only indication that it was a police car its cherry, still mutely flashing.

She never asked to see his badge.

Once inside the car, he closed the door behind her. The windows and doors had no handles—it looked as if they had been broken off. A mesh grille separated the back seat from the front. The interior smelled like corn chips, the floor littered with empty soda and beer cans. The seat was ripped.

A second officer got in and sat beside her, pulled his door shut by the edge. The badge on his chest said MURPHY. A short-cropped beard obscured half his face.

Murphy banged on the screen and the car began to move.

"Don't you want to know my address?" she asked the man beside her.

"Sure. You said Queens."

"Right, Astoria."

He leaned forward. "She lives in Astoria."

The officer driving nodded.

"Do you want my address?" Zoey's breath quickened. Pulse accelerated, and she couldn't figure out why.

Murphy stared out the window.

"But—" But what? Maybe she was pissing them off. Maybe they'd get pissed off enough to dump her somewhere in Brooklyn.

Leaned back and slumped against the seat, watched the midtown traffic trickle by, hypnotized by the nonstop rush hour traffic, pedestrians crossing against red lights, carefully maneuvering in and out of cars like pinballs. Her thoughts drifted to the confrontation with the homeless man, how he'd accosted her, how fortunate she was the police just happened to show up. Wasn't that good luck?

It finally clicked, suddenly realized why she felt uncomfortable. She glanced out the window and noticed that they were heading north on the East River Drive, not even close to the Queensborough Bridge, the way home.

Leaned into the mesh grille, wrapped her fingers in the wire. "This isn't the way. Where are you going?"

"Sit back and relax," Murphy said.

Traffic had thinned out and they were driving the speed limit. The city was disappearing behind them at an alarming rate as they passed Yankee Stadium and headed toward the George Washington Bridge. Bile choked its way into Zoey's throat. Her heart pounded.

Still they drove, crossing the bridge into New Jersey. After a while the driver made a series of turns down empty streets, onto back roads, until they reached a deserted area, an abandoned plant.

Zoey squashed herself against the door. Tried to scream but her lungs were frozen.

Fake Officer Murphy smiled. "Take it easy. We're not going to hurt you." He reached toward her and she cringed. "Look, you can make this easy, or not. You wanna be a pain in the ass?"

They never tried to hide their identity. Even if she cooperated, why wouldn't they kill her? She could pick them out of a line-up.

The car stopped rolling, and Murphy said, "Let's go."

She sucked air, threw back her head and screamed. "No! No, please!"

Murphy took her arm, and she wrapped her fingers in the mesh, bloodless fingers gripping for life, willing to relinquish only if chopped off.

He reached around behind her and brought his hand down over her face, covering her nose and mouth with a rag. Her fist flew wild, trying to connect with his nose, head, any part of his body. But then her body relaxed and collapsed on him, fingers loosening their death-grip on the wire. Somewhere beneath was a layer of panic, but she drifted away from it. It struggled to resurface, but for now, bliss.

"The hell did you use?" The driver opened her door and caught her before she slumped to the ground.

"Just something to mellow her out, Jason. She's still with us for now."

"Good. Then she can walk. I'd hate to have to carry this one."

Jason laughed. He poked Zoey in her side. "Come on, princess, get out."

Brain fog blocked thoughts of resistance and she groggily lifted her head. Slowly she slid across the seat and fell out the door when she tried to stand.

The men laughed.

"I love watching them on this stuff," Jason said. "Look at her—she can't even stand."

On her hands and knees, Zoey moved, groping for something to hold onto, blindly searching for a rock or a stick to use as a weapon.

"She'd better get used to that position," Murphy said, and both men cracked up.

"Hey, there it is," Jason said.

Zoey lifted her head, saw the van heading toward them from the distance. Tipped over on her side, physically unable to struggle any more, but her brain continued to scramble for a way out.

The van pulled up, and Zoey saw Jason talking to the driver. Out of desperation her head was clearing, charged by pure adrenaline, a fight for life.

Murphy, Jason, and a third man circled her.

"She can walk," Jason said.

The van driver shrugged. "Not a problem. Let's get her in the back."

Struggles against the men who pulled her to her feet were weak, half-hearted. Still dazed, disoriented, she offered little resistance. Roughly they shoved her into the back of the van, pushing her onto a stained mattress that reeked of stale tobacco and wet dog. They flipped her on her back and secured her arms and legs with restraints fastened to the sides of the van. Tugged on the straps, her mind focusing, panic rising.

Van driver hovered over her and flicked a syringe. Swabbed her upper arm and warned her to stay still. There was no longer any use in resisting, and a needle broken off in her arm would make things worse. Eyes closed, head rolled back, Zoey sobbed as she felt the prick of the needle, felt the liquid burn its way into her bloodstream, and moments later she drifted off.

Chapter 2

The cell, unfamiliar and dreary. Dark, and dank, steeped in humidity. Dripping sounds, like a leaking pipe.

Terror such as this was foreign to her. Had never known true fear before, fear that ripped her bowels to shreds, blurred her vision. She thought she'd known fear before—walking along a deserted side street in Queens, being followed by a group of drunk young men—but she'd been wrong. The terror now was palpable, and it stole her breath, made her nauseous. The overwhelming sensation that death was imminent stole her last bits of sanity.

Afraid to call out. Afraid not to. Her clothing was missing, replaced by a long T-shirt that stretched to cover her knees. No underwear, no shoes. Jewelry missing.

Crept across the small cell and reached the locked bars. Gave them a push, hoping they were unlocked. No such luck.

The hallway outside the cell was bathed in darkness, sparsely illuminated by dim sconces along the walls. Whoever had locked her inside knew a thing or two about atmosphere.

Every serial killer movie she'd ever seen came back to haunt her, and she was sure that some hatchet-wielding psychopath would show at any moment. She fell back on the cot and sobbed, prayed for her nightmare to end. Curled up in a ball, tried to shrink, make herself so small that she would just fold up.

Had to calm down. Think back to what happened . . . flashes of the van, of men staring down at her. Flashes of a cop. Her memory was spotty, her head reeled. Did the cop show up before or after the guys with the van? Couldn't remember. Where the hell were her clothes?

Where the hell was she?

A banging sound, like a heavy door being thrown open, crashing against a wall. Footfalls, heels against pavement. She glanced at the floor—concrete.

They were coming. Her body shook.

The footsteps stopped and she looked up. A man and a woman stood on the other side of the cell. The man, a police officer. The woman, dressed in a lab coat.

"Miss Masterson?" the woman asked, consulting the clipboard in her hands.

Zoey sobbed, nodded.

"I'm Dr. Chambers. I hope we haven't alarmed you."

The officer unlocked the cell door.

"Please follow me," the doctor said, extending her hand.

Zoey glanced at it. Looked at the doctor's unkempt crop of hair, at the collar upturned at one corner. "Where are my clothes?" Slowly she stood and headed toward the exit.

"I'll explain everything to you. What do you remember?"

The air was cooler the farther down they walked, headed toward the light at the end of the hall. The corridor was lined with cells, all empty, all dark.

"I don't remember anything," Zoey said. Cold bare feet slapped the concrete.

Dr. Chambers nodded for the officer to leave. "In here, please." She led Zoey into a small medical exam room beside the cells.

"You were brought in unconscious. Do you remember anything at all?"

"No . . . Nothing really."

"We believe you might have been sexually assaulted but wanted to wait until you were awake before doing the exam." She patted the table. "Up here, please."

This wasn't a good idea. Zoey didn't remember a sexual assault, and she didn't feel as though she'd suffered through one. Leaving seemed like a better idea. She could see her own doctor. And if she'd been assaulted, why did they have her in a cell and not a hospital? In a dark, dirty—

"Zoey?" Dr. Chambers took her elbow, and Zoey, still stunned, still overwhelmed, climbed onto the gynecological exam table.

"Feet here." Chambers lifted Zoey's feet, guided them to the metal stirrups. A soft material was draped around her ankles.

Zoey sat up. "No, I don't think—"

Ignoring her, near Zoey's head now, Chambers took Zoey's hands and lifted them above her shoulders. "Hold on to the grips."

"The what? Please . . . I want to get down." More soft material draped around her wrists. Zoey craned her neck. The doctor was securing Velcro bindings.

"What are you doing?" Her lip trembled. The room suddenly felt bitter cold.

Chambers didn't respond. She took a pair of shears and sliced the front of Zoey's shirt from neck to crotch.

"What are you doing?" she repeated, heart palpitating, body trembling. Tried to move but her wrists and ankles were securely fastened. Chambers disappeared behind her.

"Dr. Chambers? Dr. Chambers!"

The doctor returned.

"Please let me go, please! Let me out of here! Why did you tie me down? What—"

Chambers jammed a gag into Zoey's mouth, the small rubber ball pressing her tongue, and secured the elastic around her head.

"You make entirely too much noise." She draped a sheet over Zoey.

Crying made breathing almost impossible with the gag in her

mouth. She retched, sucked air through her nostrils.

"Be right back."

Fear shrouded her, smothered her breath. Her temples throbbed. This was impossible. This wasn't happening.

Chambers returned with the cop. Only now he wasn't a cop. Now he wore a white coat as well.

"Set up the legs," he told Chambers. "I'll start with the breast exam."

There was always that remote chance that this was still legitimate, that for some reason they needed to bind and gag her to effectively do this type of exam. It was possible that they would release her, tell her they were sorry, send her home now, time to go home, over now, it was all a mistake.

Chambers held a plastic tube fitted with braces. Pried Zoey's knees apart. The tube acted as a block, kept her legs widely separated, her knees resting in the braces.

He removed the sheet, separated the material of the torn shirt, exposed her full breasts.

Zoey's eyes bulged and she panted into the gag. His hands were large and soft, and they expertly roamed her breasts, gently squeezed the nipples, pressed the tissue in a move that was more medical than sexual assault.

"She's fine." Then he reached across her chest, toward the tray just beyond her sight. Pulled it closer.

The contents of the tray made her scream into the gag.

Picked up two clamps, rubber-tipped devices that looked like scissors. Fastened them to her nipples and turned the knob, increasing the tension. Pain shot through every nerve ending in her breasts, tore through the rest of her body. Flailed wildly on the table, tried to pull her hands out of the straps, threw back her head and screeched uselessly.

Eyes pleaded with him, begged him for help, for compassion.

He smiled. "It only gets better, honey. Trust me."

Chambers snorted, grinned. "Ready down here."

"What about the gag?"

"What about it? You want to listen to her screams?"

"You know I like it," he said, caressing Zoey's tender breast.

Chambers shrugged. "Do what you want. But if she gets too loud, I'm not staying."

Sobs choked her, and her face was flushed with sweat, wet with tears.

He leaned into her. "I'm Ted, by the way. Listen, Zoey, I want to take off your gag. I don't care if you cry, I don't care if you scream in blessed agony. In fact, I like that. But what I won't tolerate is mindless blabbering, begging and shit like that. Understand?"

She nodded.

"I'm not sure that you do." He reached out and flicked a clamp, sending a pulsing wave of agony through her breast. "I can make it unpleasant for you, Zoey. I can cause you a great deal of pain. If you say one word—one word at all—the gag goes back in and I apply even tighter pressure to your tits. We clear?"

Yes, it was clear.

"Good. I think we understand one another. And Zoey, for the record, screaming and crying are perfectly acceptable."

Chambers sat by the desk, crossed her arms over her chest.

He unhooked the gag and pulled it out of her mouth.

Gasped, sucked air. Her first inclination was to talk, to scream, to beg him to stop. But she believed what he'd said and stopped herself before any words came out of her mouth.

He walked toward her feet, stood between her legs. "Hang on," he said, sliding the table in beneath her so that her butt now rested on the edge. Rolled the table beside her head toward the lower part of the table.

His fingers were inside her anus first, lubricating it. Then inside her vagina. More moisture, more lubrication.

She squeezed her eyes shut, tried to pull her legs together but the tube between her knees made it impossible.

Her sight was obscured and she couldn't see what he removed

from the tray.

"Oh—you want to see? Okay." He held up a long, thin vibrator. She puffed out her cheeks, knowing she could handle that, if he planned to rape her with that thing.

Instead, he slowly inserted it into her anus. Words formed on her lips, almost escaped, but "no" came out as "Nuhhhh . . . ", and he glanced up, smiled, shook his head, slapped a piece of surgical tape over her anus.

"So far so good. Having fun yet?"

She wished she would go numb. Wished she would drop dead on the table.

"Here's where it gets trickier." He picked up a metal tool. "Speculum." He lubricated it and pushed it inside. The vibrator rested against her colon, pressed against her vagina, and the speculum spread her, collided with the bulge in her anus. Searing pain consumed her, and her legs spasmed, the too-large speculum feeling as though it were tearing her apart.

"Just having a look, Zoey." He prodded her thighs and then she felt his fingers fiddling with the speculum, and her body fought against it, tried to reject the foreign object. Muscles flexing, clenching, stomach churning.

Ted glanced at Chambers across the room. "I think . . . this speculum might be a little too big." But he pushed harder, forced it further in, and Zoey groaned, body straining against the pressure, eyes squeezed shut against the pain.

She quivered with relief when he finally removed it.

"Good," he said quietly. "There's hope for you. You just might survive your stay with us."

Droplets of sweat trickled between her breasts and down the lumps and folds of her belly. She looked down at Ted.

Stiff penis in hand, he worked it, stroked it. Shocked, Zoey stared at the ceiling, counted the network of tiles. Never expected to see that. As bad as this was, she never expected that he would—

Felt his hands on her knees but refused to look. Stared instead at the wall, at the picture hanging there, Geddes babies in a bathtub, cherubic smiles, soap bubble beards. Maybe he'd stop, maybe he wasn't going to—

The tube between her legs was removed. He rammed her with his cock, and she screamed, "God, no!" and as the words were out of her mouth she was sorry, wished she could take it back, hoped he didn't mean what he'd said.

He fucked her hard, smashed brutally against her cervix, every thrust bringing a new bout of pain. Leaned into her, removed the clamps from her nipples. Her body was a contradiction—relief for her breasts, agony everywhere else.

But he squeezed her nipples hard, pulled them toward him. She tried to follow, lifted her ribcage as far as she could but he yanked until she thought he was trying to rip them off her body.

She wailed. He pulled and twisted, his thrusts increasing in speed and intensity, faster and faster until he moaned, grunted, leaned into her for an eternity.

He lay on top of her and then pushed against her stomach, lifted himself up. He pulled his penis out of her and slapped it against her thigh, emptying the last droplets of cum, wiped the sweat off his forehead.

"Did you think I was kidding?" he asked breathily. "You'll want to learn one thing around here, Zoey. When someone says something, you'd better listen. You'll do a lot better if you remember that." He pulled up his pants.

Chambers stood up and approached them. "Nice, Ted. A little rough on the tits I thought. But nice."

He laughed. "Yeah, well."

"All right," Chambers said. "Who's next?"

From the shadows behind Zoey's head two men appeared. She struggled against the restraints, a feral response, born of reaction and not reason.

The two men had already pulled out their penises and were stroking themselves.

"Hey!" she screamed. "No!" Looked from face to face, searched for a sign of sanity and found none.

One stepped between her legs.

"Hang on a sec, John," Ted said. He stuffed the gag back inside her mouth and then reapplied the nipple clamps. "She's being punished for talking. The only time those clamps come off is to cause more pain."

"You got it," John said. "Hey—what's this? I wanted to fuck her ass."

"Not yet," Ted said. "Pick another orifice."

Her legs were pried apart and she was raped.

Half an hour later, Zoey was dragged back down to her cell.

Chapter 3

She lay in the dark, quivering, her vagina twitching and spasming like a separate life form, no longer part of her body. She wondered what she'd done wrong. Something terrible to justify this happening to her. Punishment for some heinous act that she couldn't recall? Because that was how this felt—like punishment.

Whispers in the dark. Church whispers, airy breaths sharing secrets. Was someone in her cell? No. Even in the darkness she knew she was alone. The cell was small, and she would have detected another presence.

"Huh-h-h'lo . . . " she whimpered.

The sound again. Tiny whisper, a puff of air. "Over here."

Zoey's knees trembled as they tried to support her weight. Every part of her body ached. Wary of the pain, she stood, hobbled the few feet to the corner of the cell. Pressed her face against the bars.

"We're not supposed to talk to you yet," the voice muttered. "Do as they say and you'll be okay."

"Who are you?" Her fingers wrapped around the cold steel. "What's happened to me? Why are they doing this?" The only response to her questions was a series of hushes, warnings to be quiet, from what sounded like a half dozen voices.

"Please," Zoey sobbed, "tell me."

No one answered. Zoey stumbled back to her cot.

Heard them talking to one another, quietly at first, their voices rising in sound and pitch. No one talked to her.

Back pressed against the stone wall, knees drawn up to her chest. She stretched the T-shirt over her legs. That frustrated ache in her heart was back, that bizarre hollow feeling that made her want to scream and cry, the feeling of dread and despair. The *not knowing* that made this worse.

How much worse could it possibly get? She'd been *raped*. Not once but repeatedly. What else could they possibly do to her? Trying not to think about it didn't work. It couldn't get worse than gang rape, could it? It was impossible to imagine anything worse.

The overhead lights blazed on, white filaments blinding her, and she blinked the vision back into her eyes. Movement down the hall as women poured through the cell doors that had clanged open.

An announcement from the end of the corridor: "Everyone out. I won't say it again."

She remembered the last time she had disobeyed and rushed after the others as they filed down the hall, her body bewailing every step.

Dressed like Zoey in long gray T-shirts, shoeless, none of the women spoke.

Her jailers, torturers, dressed in black, leaning against the wall at the head of the crowd. They brandished whips, and some slapped the handles into their palms. One wielded a billyclub.

A guard grabbed Zoey's arm on her way out the door. "You're new. Do what you're told and you might survive your stay here."

"My stay?"

The woman who had spoken was around Zoey's height but was about forty pounds lighter. How easy it would be for Zoey to overpower her . . . but she didn't like the odds. The outside corridor was crowded with these guards.

The woman poked a finger into Zoey's collarbone. "Never speak unless given permission. Understand?"

Zoey swallowed, nodded.

"This is where you eat, and where you get your assignments."

Assignments? So many questions . . . She pleaded with her eyes, begging to speak, was ignored.

The room was arranged cafeteria-style, banquet tables with seats for ten. She was ushered into a food line and handed a tray. She sure as hell didn't have much of an appetite.

In the corner of the room sat the medical team that had gang-raped her. Blood drained from her head and she staggered back, grasping the edge of a table. Her legs trembled, then betrayed her, dropping her to her knees on the linoleum. Her tray clattered to the floor, the food spilling.

Two men flanked her, grabbed her arms, pulled her back to her feet. When they looked in the direction she stared, they laughed.

"You'll get used to it, sweetheart." The man, so young, such a baby face, deceitfully cherubic, playfully slapped her cheek. "Sit down. I'll bring you some food."

At the table, she searched faces, women with hair plastered to their scalps, appalling welts on faces and forearms and legs, pus oozing from gashes, swollen lips and cobalt bruises mottled on cheeks, beneath eyes. They spoke to one another but ignored Zoey, even when she tried to join in their conversations.

Another tray of food was set in front of her, but the contents were unappealing. She drank the coffee.

The man who brought her the tray sat beside her, crossed his leg over his knee. "Hi, Zoey," he said, toothy grin. "You'll be seeing a lot of me. I'm James. I run the place." When he extended his hand, she hesitantly shook it, revulsion exploding on her flesh. "Just do what you're told and you'll be okay."

She blinked. He was the third or fourth person to say that to her. Just how long were they planning to keep her there? Where in Hell was she?

"I'm going to give you your first assignment. First give me your wrist."

She hesitated, then slowly extended her hand toward him.

He slipped a leather bracelet over her wrist and snapped it shut. "See? It's not always about pain. I'll tell you something else, Zoey—don't ever hesitate like that again. Not everyone is as understanding as I am. Clear?"

Lines of communication had been reduced to a series of head jerks, and she nodded.

"Good! First assignment—report to Room One. You have ten minutes."

The room began to clear. Women limped into the hallway. She studied the bracelet. Simple leather. Metal ring suspended on the outside against the back of her hand. The ends were clamped shut; this thing wasn't going anywhere.

Room One then. Christ. The trembling started again. Where was everyone going? She wondered what would happen if she just stayed there. He'd given her ten minutes. What if she took twelve? Fifteen? Two hours? The dread of wondering what was in Room One . . . was it worse than the punishment waiting for her if she disobeyed?

Legs weak, protesting against carrying her, she followed the group, in search of Room One.

Chapter 4

Down a corridor painted in soft beige tones, simple art prints adorning the walls, Zoey slowly passed door after door. Most were marked in number only and began with Number Twelve. The numbers descended, even on one side, odd on the other, spaced widely apart. She was likely on the right track, with Room One at the far end of the corridor. Her bowels felt rubbery as she slowly made her trek down the endless hallway, studying the layout, searching for a way out.

A few doors were labeled more bizarrely. Room Six—BDSM. Room Five—Surveillance. Room Nine . . . Her head snapped back when she read the sign on Room Nine. Room Four—Punishment.

Punishment? Her breathing slowed, and her hands felt clammy. *Jesus God Almighty, they've to be kidding!* Where was the exit? Maybe she could get out, could find a stairwell somewhere. She passed Room One, kept going toward the end of the hall. No doors, no sign of an exit. She wrapped her arms around herself.

No alternative it seemed. She backtracked to Room One and stared at the closed door. Reached up . . . pulled her hand back. Couldn't do this, couldn't bring herself to knock. The corridor was deserted—maybe now was the time to search for that way out. There had to be an exit.

But what if she disobeyed? What would they do to her? Even worse, what if the exit was on the other side of that door? Maybe they were going to let her leave.

She tapped, and no one answered. Knock again or turn and get the hell out of there? She tapped again. Tried the knob, which turned easily in her hand.

Poked her head inside the dark room.

"You're two minutes late." A male voice. Soft. Familiar. James.

The breath she'd been holding poured out of her lungs. A smile formed on her lips. He'd been kind to her, in a way. She trusted him as much as she was able to trust anyone in this place. He'd looked so gentle, his blonde hair falling over one eye, downy like swan feathers.

"Come on in, Zoey."

She entered the room, her eyes fighting to adjust to the darkness.

"Close the door." He cleared his throat. "This is Room One, the Introduction room. I gave you more than enough time to get here, Zoey. It's a one minute walk from the cafeteria, yet you managed to be late anyway. I was kind to you, was I not?"

She nodded.

"Speak when I ask you a question. I can't hear your head rattle, Zoey."

"Yuh-yes," she whispered, her heart thudding, sweat trickling down her neck, down the back of her knees. Tried in vain to make him out but there was no light, nothing to focus her eyes on.

"You've been bad. Haven't you, Zoey?"

Bad? No! What was he saying?

"Answer me, Zoey."

"Bad?" Her voice cracked.

"You're learning some hard lessons. But you have to learn to do as you're told. We can't have chaos around here."

That now-familiar dread returned. She felt rather than saw them approach. Hands on either side of her grabbed her arms.

She screamed, tried to pull away.

James calmly said, "You're only making it worse. Do as you're instructed. Do you understand?"

"Yes!" she sobbed. Gave up the fight, waited for them to lead her.

Her T-shirt was lifted over her head, and she stood naked in the darkness, arms and hands trying to shield her body. Then her arms were lifted above her head, her wrists pushed into shackles, clamped shut.

The lights began to slowly brighten, as if on a dimmer switch. The room was crowded with guards flanking the perimeter. Staring at her naked in the center of the room.

James approached and eyed her body. Despite what they were doing to her, she felt a fierce embarrassment, a hatred of being seen naked. Her thick stomach exposed, heavy breasts, fat thighs.

He reached up, flicked a nipple, then lowered his head to it and sucked. "See? This could have been simple. This was supposed to be introductions, a tour of the facility. But you've failed your first test, Zoey. You just keep disobeying. Why is that?"

She moaned, stared into emerald eyes that seemed so kind. So deceptive, so horrible the secrets they hid so well. This was not a kind man, this was a psychopath.

"Answer me!" he yelled, veins bulging on his neck like thick rope, and roughly squeezed a nipple.

She screamed, tried to back away from him. "I don't know! I'm sorry!"

Calmed down, smiled again. Hefted both breasts in his hands. "You don't know." Kneaded them like mounds of dough. "How does this feel? Good?"

She looked away. "No."

He fondled them, squeezed and kissed and licked. Then he let go, and walked away.

"Okay," he said, but not to her.

Two men approached her, and took over where James had left

off.

One in front grabbed her breasts, flicked the nipples with his tongue. Reached down and slid his fingers between her lips, prying them open, his thumb massaging her clit.

She tried to back away but bumped into the man behind her. She opened her mouth—

James shook his head. "Not a word, Zoey. Not one single word."

Anger overshadowed the embarrassment, but she couldn't react. Heat spread on her cheeks. Something hard poked her, rubbed against her ass. Hands slid between her legs, moist now because of the bastard playing with her breasts and clit. She gasped as the one behind her slipped his fingers inside her pussy and finger fucked her, then followed with his cock, pushing himself from behind.

Awkward, painful. He rammed the inside of her vagina at a bizarre angle, unable to insert himself in fully. Rough touches. His thick arms wrapped around her stomach, held her in a death grip.

The man in front sucked her tits, his lips hanging from one like a bloated parasite. He kicked her ankles further apart and guided his swollen member inside her. She tried to move away, to bring her legs closer together. His stomach pressed hers, and his fingers pried apart her labia. Pushed hard against her, fighting for space in her already full vagina. Pushed harder until the tearing pain made her shriek, made her swing her arms and shove her torso against him. But he was inside her now, fucking against the other cock, stretching her tortured canal, digging deeply within agonized places.

She writhed, tried to push them out. Burning, shredding pain. Hatred and shame made a grotesque marriage.

They battered harder, faster, sliced her vagina raw, their fucking a practiced rhythm. Seconds apart they came, grunted, leaned into her. A soupy blood and cum concoction tricked down her thigh.

"Good job, guys," James said, clapping them on the shoulders.

He held Zoey's breast. "Think you're finally learning?"

Before she could stop herself, before she gave herself even a split-second to think about what she was doing, she spit in his face.

He stepped back, clearly startled, wiped the spittle off his cheek. Stared at her for a moment before he reached up and released her from the manacles.

"I guess you think this is some kind of game. You think you're being defiant, but you're not." He pulled her into him, pressed their bodies together. Placed his foot behind her ankles and tripped her, dropping her to the mat. Fell on top of her, ground his groin into hers. Held her arms above her head with one hand, and reached down with the other to violate her, most of his hand inside her vagina.

"This is no fucking *game*, Zoey. Fun time is over. I've had it with your bullshit."

He removed his hand and wiped it on his pants. To the men who had raped her he said, "Take her to Room Four. I'll be there shortly."

Room Four? Her mind raced back to the signs on the doors —and she remembered Room Four, because it was marked with something other than a number.

Room Four had been marked *Punishment*.

A screaming and kicking Zoey was dragged out of Room One.

Chapter 5

They dragged her down the hall by her wrists because her legs refused to function. After what she had been through, the rape and torture and humiliation, the idea that something worse was waiting for her in Room Four paralyzed her.

"Please," she sobbed as they struggled to haul her down the corridor. They stopped, but just long enough to try to force her to stand. On her knees she wailed, begged them to stop. They snagged her wrists and hauled her on her stomach.

Room Four was the next door over.

"Stop."

The men turned toward the voice.

James approached, hand on his hip. "Maybe she's learned her lesson this time."

Zoey nodded, wiped her runny nose on the back of her wrist. Slumped on the floor, barely aware of her nudity, feeling like a death row prisoner pardoned at the last minute.

James tossed a T-shirt at her, then knelt beside her. "Go get cleaned up. Report back to me at noon, in the cafeteria. Do you understand what that means? You have an hour and twelve minutes. Would you like to guess what will happen if you're a minute late?"

She started sobbing.

He stood up, laughed. "Exactly. Now go. Get out of here."

She scrambled to her feet. One of the men showed her to the bathroom.

The tiled floor felt good against her throbbing flesh. She drew her legs up, wrapped her arms around her knees and hugged them, sobbing. Sat like that for a while, keenly aware of the time, the clock above the door clicking off the seconds. She had no intention of being late.

On wobbly legs she stood, staring at her face in the mirror, fingertips tracing the outline of rough, red patches and blotches, wrinkles where just two days ago there hadn't been any. Her blue eyes were puffy from crying, her nose red and sore. Bruises tattooed on her jawline where she had been roughly handled. She examined her body, touched her battered, tender breasts. Swollen, raw labia, vagina alive with burning pain.

Using a stack of paper towels she moistened under the tap, she gently wiped between her legs and down her thighs, cleaning away streaks of blood and sperm. The T-shirt that she pulled on again stretched to her knees.

Eleven forty-five. She gave herself lead time and headed back to the cafeteria.

Women like the living dead ambled past her in the corridor, their eyes downcast, their mouths knit tightly shut. The cafeteria was filling fast. She glanced around at the women, their bodies covered in bruises and blood. They seemed strangely calm, as if this was part of a routine, as if they were used to it. Once inside they relaxed, smiled, chatted easily with one another.

James showed up promptly at noon. Seated several feet away from the door, Zoey overheard him asking the guard stationed there if everyone was in attendance. The guard, sporting a blackjack and a whip, nodded.

"Much better, ladies," he said to the roomful of women. "No problems. Just the way I like it."

Women smiled, as if grateful for this snippet of praise. Others swallowed, visibly nervous. Zoey could almost hear their hearts beating.

"Assignments after lunch, as usual." He looked directly at Zoey. "I suggest you all be prompt."

After being rushed through a food service line, Zoey took a seat with a small group of women.

The woman across from her brushed her cropped orange hair out of her eyes and dropped her fork against the plate. "You're new. We're allowed to talk to you now. I'm Lisa."

"I'm Zoey." She pulled apart a slice of wheat bread. "So what the hell's going on? What *is* this place?"

Lisa smiled sadly, the large purple bruise on her cheek stretching. Dots of blood were spattered along her arm. "It's Hell, Zoey. We're in Hell."

The women within hearing distance nodded.

Lisa picked up her fork and poked the contents of her tray. "They do experiments here. They say it's for research."

"Everyone in this place is . . . big," Zoey said. "You know?"

Lisa nodded. "They seem to think it's a fair price for the torture they put us through. They call it an extreme weight loss method, and James believes he's doing us and the world a service."

"You're kidding . . . " Zoey said. What little appetite she'd had was gone. "What sort of experiments?" Her breath quickened, not really wanting to hear Lisa's answer.

She shook her head, her skin tone losing pigment until she was the shade of baby powder. "You'll see. I'm sorry, but you'll see. Just do what they tell you, Zoey. It makes it easier. Do what they say and maybe they won't . . . "

"Won't what?"

But Lisa didn't answer.

On her way out the door, the guard with the whip and the clipboard grabbed Zoey's wrist and looked at the leather bracelet. "Report to Room Two. You have five minutes."

Zoey glanced at the bracelet, noticed the number stamped into the leather.

"I'd suggest you haul your ass. Wouldn't be smart for you to be late again."

Whatever they were planning, she couldn't take any more. Her groin was an inferno, tender and bloated; she could barely walk. The thought of more of the same was too much to handle.

Zoey slowly approached Room Two. No sign on the door other than the number, no indication of what might be inside.

Unlocked, the knob turned easily in her trembling hand. She wondered why they bothered with doors at all. Probably to keep sound out. Or in.

"Right on time," a man said, and this time it wasn't James.

The room was small, adorned with chains and cuffs suspended from walls, the lighting dark and moody, the smell musky and heavy, ingrained, living in the leather and wood of the tools and furniture inside. Many of the cuffs were already in use, women naked and hanging, or propped against walls. Full breasts and fuller bodies, bruises and cuts and scratches like erratic tattoos.

The guard approached her. A few inches taller than Zoey and more than a few pounds lighter, built like a biker or swimmer. His brown hair was neatly trimmed in an almost bowl shape on his head.

"I'm Tony," he said, and before she could answer him, added, "Shirt off." Bypassed her, as if speaking to her had been an afterthought. She licked her lips, took a breath, pulled off her shirt. Held it in a ball in front of her chest. He came back and said, "I'll try to go easy on you, but I do have a few routines that are mandatory."

She opened her mouth to respond but he cut her off. "I don't want to hear it. No talking. Come with me."

She followed him across the room, passing women being whipped, others being slapped and paddled. Strangely quiet, eyes closed, the impact of their pain apparent on their strained faces, bodies laced with puckered scars and purple, dribbling lacerations.

In the middle of the room, like the center ring in a sideshow display, a woman was strapped to a device the likes of which Zoey had never seen before. Had never imagined. Her back supported by a padded bench, her body upright, she was tied spread-eagle, her arms locked behind her back. The chair was mechanical and dipped forward with agonizing slowness, impaling her on an oversized phallus, pushing her onto it fully, then slowly pulling her back out. The woman's eyes were open but weren't focused on anything in particular; had in fact a dead glaze about them, a woman who had lived through one trauma too many and had given up.

Tony saw where Zoey's attention was riveted. "That's the rape chair," he said, taking her wrist. "She's going to be there for a while."

They stopped in front of a pommel horse, leather covered, about three and a half feet high from where it was anchored to the floor. Two men, holding whips and leather straps. Another woman Zoey recognized from the cafeteria—she thought her name was Marie—waited as well, her head slightly cocked, body visibly trembling as if somehow in this murky heat she felt cold.

The one with the whip grabbed Zoey's arm and pushed her face-first into the pommel horse. She'd seen this piece of gymnastics equipment before in the Olympics, had even seen it in high school gym class ten years earlier. This one was similar, lower to the floor it seemed than the ones used by gymnasts, but the same bullet shape.

"Bend over," he said, and she did. Grabbed the rings in the center of the horse and laid between them. Submission didn't come easily for her, and the anger burned her cheeks, made her want to reach back and rip his throat out. He gently kicked her feet farther apart. She clutched the rings but the other guard took her wrists and directed them straight out over her head.

Flanking her were Marie and Lisa. They were told to stretch across the horse, lying on either side of Zoey, their arms stretched toward her legs.

The hilt of the bullwhip was dragged along Zoey's back, up and down the length of her legs, between her thighs, trailed along the outer edges of her swollen labia. She shuddered as it was forced between her vaginal lips, as it slightly penetrated her cunt. Sweat popped out on her forehead, and her stomach flipped. He pulled it out, and she could sense him moving around behind her.

On Zoey's left, Marie puffed out her cheeks, eyes rolling, exposing only the whites. Breasts mashed to the leather surface of the horse. Her eyes then shut so tightly Zoey saw tiny veins popping out on the lids. Behind her, the guard massaged his cock, worked it, the tip glistening with spit or lubricant. He reached between her legs, and Marie gripped the pommel horse with stark white fingers.

Lisa stared vacantly ahead, oblivious to the vibrator violating her. Tongue jutting, eyes squinting, waiting for the attack to end. Long brown hair dusted the surface of the horse, her body moving in concert with his.

So engrossed by what was happening beside her she was unprepared for the first stinging crack of the whip across her ass. She screamed, tried to turn around.

"Don't move, Zoey." He grunted, struck again.

Biting pain enraged her, and she tried to protect herself with her hands. Unrelenting blow after blow, like a swarm of stinging hornets. Tears streamed down her face. The women beside her sobbing, moaning.

The beating stopped. His hands roamed her inflamed ass, massaged her, as if trying to drive the whipmarks into her skin. Fingers prodded, separated her folds, pried her open, drove the digits inside. His cock followed his fingers and he fucked her hard, rammed her into the pommel horse. Every thrust anguish, every movement slicing her deeper.

Grunted, pulled out, slapped her on her ass, told her not to move.

Marie had paled, looked like she would pass out. Her attacker didn't seem to be losing speed and fucked her harder, yelled with each thrust, grabbed her hair and yanked her head back.

"Oh, God!" Marie screamed, her mouth thrown open, jaw locked in pain. She clutched at the pommel horse as if trying to scale it. Zoey reached back, clutched Marie's hands but received a whip crack across her wrists for the effort. Finally Marie succumbed, silently endured the rape. It wasn't as if she had a choice.

The guards finished and walked away. Zoey exchanged a glance with the women, a look of futility and desperation.

Tony returned, stood with arms folded. Shook his head, clicked his tongue. "What's the first rule of fight club?"

The women looked perplexed, but Zoey's heart sank.

"Anyone?" Tony asked. "Feel free to blurt out the right answer."

"No talking," Zoey whispered. "That's the first rule."

"Ding ding ding! Give that lady the Cracker Jack prize." He leaned into the edge of the pommel horse and stared into Marie's eyes. "Care to guess who broke the rule?"

The sorrowful wail that poured out of Marie made the hair on the back of Zoey's neck prickle.

"Go now," he said. "Those nice men by the door are waiting to take you to Room Four."

Zoey caught her breath, wanted to scream but her lungs

seized up. The guards approached Marie and dragged her screaming out into the hall. The door slammed shut behind them.

Tony took Zoey's elbow and led her to another part of the room, past the screams and moans and whimpers. Pointed toward the floor. Two metal hoops, shoulder width apart, jutted from wood slats. Pushed to her knees, shoved forward, her hands forced between the loops and locked in. A leather hood was draped over her head, the eyes, nose, and mouth holes zipped closed. Air was fleeting, and Zoey panicked, struggled frantically but her wrists were securely fastened.

Someone grabbed her head and held her steady. Unzipped the small hole beneath her nose. Air gushed in. Other senses were cut off, and she felt that she was no longer part of the world.

Her legs were forced apart, cushions placed beneath her knees. Felt . . . someone at her swollen, aching vagina . . . wet, licking, a tongue lapping at her pussy. Fingers prodded, flicked her clit, explored. Pushed inside her, all the way in, so deep, many long thin fingers in and out. She didn't want to feel this, didn't want any sensation from their touch, but her body had its own agenda. She tried to fight the carnal feelings but couldn't. The fingers fucked her harder, deeper still, worked her cunt, a second hand diddled her clit, squeezed it between thumb and forefinger, rolled it, hot plumes of breath tickled it. Licking and sucking, and as much as she tried to fight it she was cumming.

A cock pulsed inside her while fingers played with her clit. They groped her tits, pulled the nipples. Lack of senses was unbearable. Sweltering heat inside the hood. One finished fucking her and another took his place, then another and another until she lost count, the number dizzying, until her knees trembled and her body ached and her vagina was a pit of fire.

The pace slowed, and she prayed they were tiring. Someone slid beneath her, awkwardly taking her from below, pushing his cock up and into her. But there couldn't be anyone beneath her, she would have felt his body. A hand brushed against her mound, a dildo held in position inside her.

Someone took her from behind again, stuffing her with his engorged dick, sharing her pussy with the dildo. Her body shuddered, tried to deal with the torment, fresh bouts of pain when she'd thought she couldn't take any more.

When he finished and pulled out she collapsed on her side, her chest heaving, fluids tricking down swollen inner thighs. They unshackled her from the floor, removed the hood.

The screams from the other women had gone unheard, distorted by the leather encasing her head. She dropped onto her back. Eyes closed, she prayed for her own death.

Chapter 6

I can help you.

In her dream, she kills Mel, over and over, each way bloodier, each way more satisfying than the last. It was Mel who precipitated these events, whether intentional or not. How could she not have known? Mel, the harbinger of torture and pain, now dead.

Zoey's hands, wrapped around the scrawny bitch's even scrawnier neck, fingers embedded in the flesh, throttled her until the bitch turned shades of red and purple, eventually blue.

James was next, and she stabbed him with a butterknife, his eyeball hanging from gristly strings flecked with gore, and he screamed in pain every time she attacked his flesh, ragged holes weeping blood, hurting him as much as he had hurt her. Hurting him more.

When she woke from this violent and fitful sleep, her head pounded, felt like a massive hangover. What she wouldn't give for a good stiff drink.

She sat up and clutched the sweat-soaked sheet. Couldn't remember who had dressed her, couldn't remember coming back to her cell. Not that nudity mattered much any more. Just about everyone had seen her naked, had seen every bit of her fat protruding, jiggling as they fucked her, being squeezed and poked and prodded like mounds of rising dough. What the hell did it matter anymore?

The burning sensation had subsided. Her fingertips came away moist and sticky, coated in some foreign substance. Assumed it was some sort of salve but couldn't tell in the darkness. She hoped it wasn't blood.

She wondered if anyone in the outside world was looking for her. Not that she had many people in her life. Parents dead, sister living a thousand miles away, and they hardly spoke any more. In the blackness she imagined Julie's face, reached out to touch the image, wanted to hold her, to be comforted by her sister.

Was there a chance the police knew where she was? A possibility that her job had been concerned when she didn't show up? There was always that hope, a persistence that she shouldn't give up.

Maybe someone was looking for her.

Every time she thought they'd reached the pinnacle of inhumanity, had tested her endurance with the most horrendous acts imaginable, they came up with something else. So now, what else could there be? Envisioning a worse scenario was impossible.

Breathing: soft moans, loud snores of exhaustion. No words save for the occasional cry in someone's sleep. The air was heavy with the smells of soap and futility. Darkness, obscuring her sight, unsure how many of the other women were also in their cells. She had tried counting heads in the cafeteria and came up with sixteen prisoners. There were almost as many rapists and torturer guards.

The clanging at the end of the corridor startled her. Clutched the sheet, pulled it up to her chin, a cotton-polyester shield.

The footsteps ended outside her cell door. She could make out a silhouette from the dim light thrown by the open door at the end of the hall.

"Let's go, Zoey," the shadow said, unlocking the cell door and throwing it open.

She followed the invisible footsteps down the corridor and into the outer hallway. Entered another door just on the other side of the exit. Climbed a short, narrow flight of stairs, reached yet another door. Cooler up here, a slight breeze brushed against her cheeks.

Ushered inside, told to sit, to not touch anything. Hands in her lap, Zoey glanced around the office. Shelves lined with books. Large globe in the corner. Framed prints hanging from the wood paneling. Could have been a college professor's office. Except . . . except for the medieval torture rack in the corner of the room, and a cage suspended from the ceiling like a twisted birdhouse, just large enough for a human head.

"Good morning, Zoey. I'm Dr. Sullivan."

His voice startled her, and the hair on her arms bristled, heartbeat quickened. He sat across from her behind the mahogany desk, steepled his hands beneath his chin in an attempt to look scholarly, as if studying her, his science project. She swallowed, wondered what he wanted, why she had been brought here.

"From New York, I see."

Nod? Smile? Cough? She didn't know how to respond.

He smiled. "You're allowed to talk in here."

She relaxed a bit, not even aware that she had.

"I'm a counselor. I'm here to help our guests emotionally."

"Guests?" she asked quietly, terrified of uttering that first word.

"I prefer the term *guests*." He lightly tugged at the tuft of hair on his cheek, as if making sure it was still attached.

Guests. *Victims is more like it*, she thought. *Prisoners.*

"We conduct research. Sexual studies, things of that nature."

She could actually feel the anger swelling, could feel the heat exploding on her cheeks. *Research*? Was he for real?

"As long as you cooperate, Zoey, your stay with us will be uneventful."

"Uneventful? I've been raped! I've been beaten and molested, fucking *tortured*. What do you consider uneventful?" She hovered over his desk, her breasts tipping the paperclip holder and the pencils in a mug stamped with some inane Best Dad Ever message.

He looked past her, and she glanced back, noticed the guard standing in the doorway.

"Sit down, Zoey," he said calmly. "You've been given permission to speak, but one more outburst like that and the session's over."

She sat, trembling hands palms up in her lap. *Session.* She wondered what his credentials were, if he even had any.

"This facility was created for the purpose of conducting research. We gauge reaction, stimulus, response, as well as neurological, biochemical, physical, and emotional reactions . . . many others. Some tests will require your being hooked up to sensors that will gauge your responses. Other tests are purely reactionary. I assure you, it's all quite harmless. Including your 'rape', as you call it. What you call rape, we call research. It's for the good of humanity, Zoey. Think of it as a humanitarian effort. It doesn't matter how you handle it anyway, because you'll eventually get over it. You'll recover."

"I can't believe what you're saying . . . " Her insides were a churning tempest but outwardly she remained calm. "How can you even think this is something I would ever simply 'get over', just because you say I should?"

He sucked his teeth, cleared his throat. "I was hoping for more enthusiasm, Zoey. You don't seem like a team player. I thought you might be interested in working for us."

Opened her mouth, closed it again. Not sure how to respond. "How?"

"As a recruiter perhaps. Like Mel. Or in some other capacity."

It couldn't be this easy. To agree to work for them seemed like her way out. She nodded. "Okay. Count me in."

He laughed, his eyes widening. "It doesn't work that way. You have to complete your stay with us first. Then we evaluate."

"And how long is my stay?"

"That all depends on you." He stood up and cleared a spot of the edge of the desk, sat in front of her. "We're giving you something in exchange for your participation in our research."

"What's that?"

"When you leave here, you're going to be thin."

How bizarre that he believed this was acceptable payment for torture. "That's the deal? I'm going through this shit because you've put me on some kind of diet?"

He returned to his seat, leaned back in the chair. "Well . . . yes. You can leave once you've lost the weight. This is why we accept larger women into the program. Nothing too big though—gets in the way of . . . research."

"Did it ever occur to you morons that gang-raping a woman would be more traumatic than her carrying around extra body weight? What kind of justification is that, anyway? You're out of your mind. And did it ever occur to you that some women *like* the way they look? Some people are happy with the way they are."

"Hell no. And certainly not you. You're in classic denial, Zoey. You were investigated before you were brought here. You've been miserable, and we can make you happy, Zoey. We can make you thin."

She was investigated? When? They picked her up shortly after her conversation with Mel. When the hell had they researched her?

He must have noticed the confusion on her face. "Oh, did you

45

think Mel's approaching you was a coincidence?"

Dry tongue slid across dry lips. Tears threatened to fall. "But it doesn't work that way . . . " she whispered. "I'm happy the way I am. I want to go home."

"You *are* home, Zoey. And it really is that simple. We've had hundreds of test subjects come through here. Very few were disappointed with the results. Jesus, most women will do anything to be thin. Do you know that a study showed that formerly overweight women would rather lose a limb than gain back the weight?"

Palmed away tears that trickled toward her mouth. "What about the others?"

"What others?"

"The few that you said were disappointed in the results."

"Oh. They're—around." He shook his head. "We're getting off track. How do you feel about being overweight, Zoey?"

Oh, but was this a trick question? Even if she hated being fat, it didn't mean she wanted to be fucked thin by being raped. "I'm not that big."

"That's true, but I know you hate it. I've seen your file. We may take extreme measures, but we get results. Our guests are happy. Our overweight guests lose weight, our corporate clients get their research."

"Corporate clients."

"Absolutely. This is big business, Zoey. Sexual research is conducted for all aspects of the industry—condoms, lubricants, sex toys, magazines, clothing, the list goes on. Haven't you ever wondered how they came up with results for an orgasm study? That was one of my favorites, by the way."

Nausea repaid a visit, stronger than before, inciting her stomach to riot. She closed her eyes, waiting for the feeling to pass.

"We're done for today. I wanted you to have some insight into this, Zoey. Maybe you'll be more cooperative now that you

understand the program. I want you to enjoy your stay here."
Lowered his head, studied the papers on his desk.

Session over.

She followed the guard down the stairs. Back in the cafeteria, James motioned for her to sit with him at his table. "Have a good visit?"

Reluctantly, she sat across from him and stared at her plate. Runny eggs and burnt toast made for a less than appealing breakfast.

"You don't seem happy, Zoey."

Her fork clattered on the plate, and she looked up at him, unsure if she was allowed to speak. But his eyes were transfixed on hers, as if anticipating her response.

"This place," she sighed through clenched teeth, "is a festering cesspool. This has been the worst experience of my life."

Tilted his head and lowered his eyes, now addressing the breasts clearly outlined through the fabric of her shirt. "So dramatic, Zoey," he whispered, glanced up again. "There have only been a handful of women I've been really attracted to. I was hoping you would enjoy being here. Spending time with me . . . How can I change your mind?"

"You can't." Her gaze matched his, unwavering, solid, hers aflame with hatred.

"I can try. You're special, Zoey. Maybe someday you'll feel the same about me." He got up and walked across the room.

She chewed a piece of toast. "Not a chance in Hell . . . " she mumbled, deciding he was more delusional and psychotic than she had given him credit for.

A few minutes later he was back. "Come with me," he said. "Leave your tray."

Jill, Kim, and several other women Zoey didn't know by name followed James to Room Eight. The walls were mirrored from ceiling to floor, the floor foam padding. Track lighting adorning the perimeter was soft, calming.

"This is what I call the touchy-feely room. It pisses me off."
He laughed, and traced the corners of his mouth with his finger
and thumb. "But I suppose it's a breather for you ladies. Robin,
you've done this room before, right?"

Robin, the guard, nightstick on her belt, was small in stature
but powerfully built, like a bulldog. Her long black hair was
pulled behind her ears and tied in a ponytail. "Yes, I have."

James left. Another guard stood vigil by the closed door.

"Shirts off," Robin said.

No one hesitated. T-shirts were removed and tossed to the
side.

Robin leaned against the wall. "Everyone pair up."

Zoey's partner was Jill. Thinner than Zoey, with apple-sized
breasts, large, dark nipples. Jill's nudity embarrassed Zoey, the
close proximity of her breasts, the sweat shining on her skin. The
other women didn't wait for further instructions and embraced,
began to explore one another.

Zoey blushed, looked away from her partner. This was
something she'd never done before, had never even considered.
There'd been one drunken frat party years ago where she'd
kissed another woman, but it wasn't something she'd
particularly enjoyed, just something she wanted to try.

"Lay down," Robin told her. She bent Zoey's knees, her feet
flat on the floor. Took Jill's hands, laid them on Zoey's body.

"Explore her," Robin said. "You've done this before. Touch
her breasts, caress her."

Jill obeyed, but mechanically, eyes squeezed tight, face
turned toward the floor.

"You're doing it wrong. She's a guest like you. This is your
chance to bring comfort to another prisoner's life, make her feel
good, feel some real happiness. Are you willing to steal that
away from her?"

Jill started to cry, turned away from Zoey.

"Jill, knock it off. Get it right, or you know what'll happen."

Using the nightstick, Robin tapped Zoey's knees, spreading them.

Jill sighed, and with a hesitant touch began to caress Zoey, to massage her breasts, her ribcage, fingertips tracing delicate patterns on her stomach and abdomen, stroked the tender flesh between her legs. She leaned over, suckled a nipple, trailed her tongue along the same route her hands had traveled.

Zoey closed her eyes and pretended that Jill was Barry. He'd dumped her when he said she'd gotten too fat, but that didn't matter now. Barry with the puppy-dog eyes and hint of facial hair that never grew no matter how hard he tried. Using him in this way was poetic justice for the way he had treated her. Feminine fingers probing her body belonged to Barry. That tongue, laying slow kisses along her stomach, dipping into her belly button, glistening traces of spit on her inner thighs—all Barry. His hands spreading her legs, soft lips separating her clefts. She tilted her pelvis, hot breath on her clit, moist tongue probing, licking, sucking. Arched her back, thrust her hips to the eager mouth, warm wet lips expertly bringing her to climax, exploring deeper and deeper until she came, until she shuddered and spasmed and came again.

The sound of Robin's voice destroyed the illusion. "Good, Jill. You're done for now. Go see if Steve wants anything." The guard at the door smiled as Jill approached him.

Zoey leaned on her elbow, breathing hard, sheen of sweat cooling on her skin. The women were fucking one another, sticky balls of flesh, some taking turns, others laying head to foot. Legs spread, women on top of women, women side by side.

Robin was removing her clothes, staring at Zoey. Smiled, slowly ran her tongue across her bottom lip.

She was aware of her nudity again, and crossed her arm over her breasts, pulled her knees together. Her head was spinning, that feeling of dread beginning at the base of her skull. "No," she blurted, "I'm supposed to—" Lifted her arm, waved it in Jill's direction. Jill was busy on the other side of the room, Steve the guard enjoying a blow job.

She looked up as Robin reached her, brandishing the nightstick, slammed it into Zoey's stomach. She grunted, doubled over. Robin pushed her onto her stomach and beat her with the club. Zoey tried to crawl away but Robin was relentless.

Zoey sobbed, her body bruised, stinging. Robin spread Zoey's legs, shoved the nightstick in and fucked her with it, yelling with every thrust, smashing it against her uterus, every blow a flash of lightening-bolt pain.

Screaming, Zoey reached down, tried to pull out the club. Robin backhanded her across her face.

"Don't move!" Pounded harder, faster, until Zoey was hysterical, the pain crippling, draining her strength, stealing her resolve.

Robin pulled out the nightstick and lay down beside Zoey. Out of breath, her hair liberated from the ponytail and stuck in sweaty clumps to her forehead and chin. "Fuck me," she said. "Get me off."

Body trembling, barely able to move, Zoey crawled over to Robin and stared at her naked body.

Robin opened her eyes. "You'd better do me the way Jill did you. You'd better get it right. I want to enjoy this."

Zoey moaned, lowered her shivering body to Robin's. With tentative fingers she reached her breasts, massaged them. Licked the nipple.

Barry has nipples, Barry has nipples, these are . . .

"You're about one second away from being fucked up the ass with my nightstick, Zoey. Do it right."

Sucked the nipple harder, rolled her palm over the other. Caressed Robin's flat stomach with dry lips, explored the area between her knees. She separated Robin's legs and positioned herself between them, lowering her head to her crotch. Couldn't do this. Couldn't bring herself anywhere near that woman's mound of pubic hair.

Her thoughts wandered, and she was twelve, at her aunt's farm. Picking apples from the neighbor's yard until she and her sister got caught and were chased by a crazy woman with a broom.

Fingers spread Robin's labia, dipped inside her pussy.

Apple trees; white blossoms and powerful, sweet fragrances, fighting the bees for possession of the tart fruit. Wind in her hair, cooling sticky sweat—

Robin grunted. "Use your mouth."

Zoey bit her lip, drew a breath. Being raped with a nightstick was worse than this. Had to think of that, the only way to get through this.

Zoey grabbed Robin's ass and lifted it, pulled her pelvis closer to her face. Tongue piercing Robin's slit, tasting the salty fluids, hot, sticky moisture sheathing her tastebuds. Flicked the lingua against the walls, mouth fucking her, hot breath tickling her fine hairs until Robin bucked, moaned, squealed in delight, pounded her fists against the padding.

Lowered her ass to the floor, sat up, leaned back on her palms. "Was that so hard? Now do Jill. I want to watch."

Chapter 7

Alone in the cells, dim sconce struggling like the flame of a dying candle. Surprised that they hadn't left her seething in total darkness.

Body damp, shirt clinging feverishly to her skin. Pushed sticky hair off her chin. Smelled her own ripeness, the unwashed odors of sweat and despair.

Now she had company. He quietly entered the cell and sat beside her on the cot.

"That wasn't supposed to happen," James said.

"Get the fuck away from me." Zoey pulled the sheet over herself.

"You must have done something to piss Robin off. She just got a little carried away."

"Fuck you." Screw their rules. She didn't have much to lose by expressing herself—what more could they possibly do to degrade her? Besides, it felt wonderful to vent.

The other cells were empty. She wondered what time of day it was, because she never knew for sure, not in this windowless torture chamber where the clocks indicated numbers but never an accurate time of day. She slept and woke as commanded but her internal clock had never felt more confused, not even during her frequent trips to and from England to visit then-boyfriend Doug in England.

"I want to go home," she moaned. "Why can't I just go home? I don't belong here. All those other women seem to be handling this, but I can't."

The sheet was draped over his leg and he pushed it aside, rested his hands on his lap, leaned against the brick wall. "They're not all handling it. Some are worse off than you. You're just not seeing it."

"That's a small comfort."

Cocked his head, studied her breasts, and with a tentative, almost shy gesture slowly trailed a finger along her arm. "Big women are beautiful," he whispered.

Fire burned in her brain. "Then why the hell do you want to make them thin?"

"It's my gift, Zoey. My way of pleasing you. I know what you want."

"You're still not getting the idea. The only way to make me happy is to let me leave this place."

He smiled. "I can't do that. But you'll only be here for a few months. Six, tops."

Six months? Her jaw muscles worked, mouth dropped open. "What?"

"That's not so long. You just need to adjust."

"I can't! I want to go now." The frustration grew, a frenzied mass trying to explode through the top of her head.

He stood, stretched his arms overhead. "Stop yelling. Maintain a civil tongue, Zoey."

But now she was sobbing, her balled-up hands pounding the mattress.

"Last chance to settle down. I do have standards to maintain."

And she heard him, heard every last word but couldn't control herself, needed this release.

"I'm giving you three seconds, Zoey. As much as I like you, I can't make exceptions, can't deviate from my standards."

Three seconds came and went, and so did James. She collapsed on her face and sobbed into the pillow.

#

Clanking metal woke her—how long had she been asleep? The cell that had been a stark gray was now without a source of light and had become as dark as a starless night sky. The light poured in from the end of the hall, and a stream of women flowed inside, entering their cells. Their voices sounded like sighs, the beating of tiny insect wings.

Zoey crept across the floor and wrapped her fingers around the bars, peered into the now-blackness of the cell beside her own. "Kim? You there?"

Conversations were minimal, their voices sounding tired. The sweet musky scent of sweat mingled with blood hung on the air, thick and pithy.

"I'm here, Zoey." Kim was beside her, on the opposite side of the bars.

"Anything going on?"

"No surprises, if that's what you mean. We were wondering what happened to you."

"After that bitch Robin attacked me, they brought me back here."

"You're okay?"

"Yeah. I guess." Zoey sighed, expelling the weight of the world from her lungs.

"Get some sleep. I'm exhausted. They really wore me out."

"I know how you feel, Kim. Try to rest."

She started to sob, her shoulders hunched into the bars. "I can't take any more, Zoey. I want to go home. I just want to die."

No words would come. Zoey empathized, held her through the bars as best as she could, until Kim sniffed and pulled away.

Hands extended for guidance in the blackness, Zoey found her cot. Curled up and fell asleep.

#

The following morning—she guessed it was morning, it could have been any time at all—Chambers paid her a visit. Medical kit in hand. Applied a cream to the area between Zoey's splayed legs. Then told her to lie on her stomach and inspected her back.

"Not too bad," Chambers said. "Some bruises, light scratches. You've been lucky so far."

Lucky.

Again in the cafeteria, ground zero, given her assignment by a guard scratching his hairless head his pencil. "You're in Room Nine today. Huh. Good luck in there."

Oh great. *Good luck?*

His face drooped, and he looked forlorn, as if he were sending her into battle unarmed. "Just . . . Remember to do what they tell you, okay?"

A cold chill gripped her colon.

"And be there by ten."

That left her less than ten minutes, so she headed down the corridor.

Good luck, the guard had said. Was he trying to scare her? It worked. Her heart thumped against her ribs. She sucked air and stepped into the dark room.

The air was damp, mildewy, sat on her taste buds. It was a peculiar claustrophobic feeling, akin to being buried alive. A metallic, salty tang filled her nostrils. Reminded her of the time she had gone deep-sea fishing with her grandfather of the coast of the Jersey shore. He'd caught a marlin, and she'd caught a baby shark. She could smell that air again now.

In the corner of the room there was a chair, more like an exam table, similar to the one they had used her first day there to rape her after her gynecological exam. This was shorter, and it also had stirrups. The line of six women moved quickly through, each having a turn in the chair, something being inserted into their vaginas.

"Zoey—let's go." Tony shoved her toward the line. When it was her turn she climbed up, sank back into the plush leather. Her feet were guided into the stirrups.

"Relax, this is nothing. Just inserting an electrode to monitor your responses." Chambers said to Ted, standing beside her, "Number 99552. Name Zoey. Lot number 8359."

"Okay, here we go." She pushed a single finger inside. Zoey barely felt it, and had been unable to see what se was inserting. Slight pressure, deep. Pulled it out, inserted another finger inside Zoey's anus, pressed against the wall.

Seven women, including Zoey, were told to strip and were ushered to the center of the room.

The guards undressed and were stroking themselves. The women were forced to the floor.

Zoey's guard wanted his dick in her mouth, and she shuddered, knowing resistance would be worse than this. She accepted him, licked the hard shaft, teased the balls with her fingers.

"Get it good and wet. Suck it." Lips kissed the tip, took as much of his swollen member into her mouth as she could. He pulled out, knelt beside her. "Turn around."

On her hands and knees. Wet fingers pawed at her pussy. But then his cheek rested against her ass, steamy breath tickling the delicate hairs, and licked her asshole. It closed up, resisted his tongue.

He plunged his spit-slicked finger inside her anus.

Around her, groans, sobs, squeals of pain. The smell of body fluids ripe, heavy.

"Spread your legs," he said, and licked her asshole again. The tip of his engorged cock poked against the tiny hole.

"No," she begged, agonized gasps stealing her voice, "not there. Please, not there."

Slowly he impaled her, half an inch at a time, a sensation that she was tearing from the inside out. Pain rippled through her body. He pulled out, a spasm of momentary relief. Drove into her again, and the agony started once more.

"Oh, God!" she sobbed. "Please stop!" Tears dripped to the floor, fingernails gouging into the padding beneath her.

A bit more until he entered her fully with one final, powerful thrust. She screamed, tried to crawl away.

Fucked her ass, pumped and pounded, clutched her hips like handles. Fondled a breast when he could, crushed it against her body, pinched sore, abused nipples. He convulsed against her and pulled out, a blood and cum mixture tricking down the back of her thigh.

Nausea captured her breath, and she collapsed on her side.

After the moaning subsided, after the cries began to die down, a guard said, "Most of you did well. Two of you did not."

Oh, no. Clamped her eyes shut, clutched her stomach.

"Zoey, Lucy. Over here, please."

Dread washed over her like acid rain. Her feet slipped in the bloody cum. Got up again and joined Lucy.

The guard handed Zoey a towel. "Wipe your ass." He cocked his head, clicked his tongue. "What the fuck is it with you two? When will you learn?"

He pointed to rings bolted to the floor. "Get down, hands and knees. Grab the rings." Similar setup to the room where she'd been forced to wear the leather hood. Their hands were snapped into the cuffs. Several feet of floor separated the two women.

Hands pulling her ankles wide apart. He chest was pushed to the floor, her ass held up in the air by someone guiding her hips. Lucy was pushed into the same position.

"Listen up, you two. If you move, not only will you have to go through this anyway, but I'll beat the shit out of you first. Clear? Answer yes or no."

Voices shaking, both said yes. Zoey wished for her death, wished the earth would open up and swallow her whole.

"Okay, we're ready," he said.

Zoey heard a door click open, heard panting breaths like an overzealous lover . . . heard the slight whines, the sniffing. Felt the cold, wet nose pressed against her groin, inspecting the blood and the torn anus. Then the nose moved further, seeking out her vagina . . . its tongue followed, lapping at her cunt.

"Oh, no . . . " Lucy moaned. "No!"

Zoey forced her mouth shut, forced herself not to say a word.

Felt paws on her lower back, then around her abdomen. The animal's large, hard penis pressed against her crotch. The shock of penetration, ragged breath harsh, uneven, arms quivering, the dog's moist panting against her back, its sharp claws digging into her flesh.

It nipped her, pushed into her, its rhythm awkward, feral.

It finally pulled out and was gone. Her wrists were unlocked and someone pulled her up off the floor, and she was pushed toward the other women.

Lucy's dog finished shortly after, but she was left in the same position. A guard removed his belt and struck Lucy, the cracks sounding like gunshots. Lucy was sobbing but not saying a word.

"If you move, Lucy, it'll only get worse. If you *speak*, Lucy, it'll get horrible. Do you understand? Yes or no?"

"Yuh-yes!" she wailed.

"Okay, we're ready."

Zoey turned her head toward the door as the dog handler entered the room. The Great Dane's cock was enormous, at least twelve inches long, several inches thick. It swayed between its legs like a massive pendulum as it trotted over, licked Lucy's crotch before mounting her.

Lucy's agonized screams pierced Zoey's ears and shredded her heart. Over the animal's guttural snarls, she heard the soft sound of Lucy's vagina tearing, like tissue paper being ripped to shreds.

The dog trotted off, leaving Lucy sobbing in a puddle of blood.

"Get her on her feet," James said, entering the room. He stood before Lucy, glared at her, then shook his head.

He wandered a few feet away and motioned for the guards to bring Lucy over, and she was secured face-up to the rings on the floor.

"Get me the Pear," he said, and Lucy began to sob, and the women beside Zoey gasped or squeezed their eyes shut.

"Please, James," Lucy moaned, panting, near hysterics. "Please don't. I swear I'll listen. I'll do whatever you say. I swear to God . . . " But her choking sobs cut off her words, and what followed next was a shrill scream that rattled through Zoey's eardrums.

James ignored her pleas and accepted the device from the guard who had retrieved it. His eyes were hard, cold slits, his lips pressed into an angry tight line.

On the floor, Lucy twitched, her knees jammed together in a futile attempt to ward off her attacker, her body twisted as if undecided which direction it desired to go.

"Spread her," he said, and Lucy howled, threw back her head.

The Pear was named for its shape, the large metallic oval head supported by a thick rod leading to its base. At the end of the rod, a lever. Metal prongs adorned the head of the Pear.

James pushed the Pear into Lucy's vagina, and Zoey could see the oversized bulb obscenely spreading the woman's tortured flesh.

Lucy thrashed, tried to slide away on the floor.

Two-fisted, he gripped the handle and began to rotate the lever. With each turn, the Pear spread Lucy further, the metal prongs catching her flesh, and she screeched, unable to escape the torment.

James turned and turned the lever until there was a hideous ripping sound, until blood poured from between Lucy's legs.

Unconscious or dead, she no longer moved. The stunned women were told to report back to the cells.

Chapter 8

Lights out for over an hour now. Zoey crept over to the bars that separated her cell from Kim's and lightly tapped the metal with her fingertips. The clink was barely audible, but in the silence of the room it was loud enough. If Kim was already sleeping she didn't want to wake her.

A minute later, Kim's fingers entwined around Zoey's on the bars. Zoey pressed her face against the cool metal.

"We have to get out of here," Zoey whispered, lofty breath carrying her message. "I've been watching them, Kim. This place is not that well guarded. And they don't even have real weapons, just clubs and whips. Those aren't lethal, not like guns and knives."

"No, Zoey, we can't. I'm scared. If we got caught . . . "

Zoey could barely make out the other woman's features, could see a flash of white when Kim blinked. A wall sconce had been left lit, throwing the dimmest shadow into the darkness. Other than that, Kim was barely a silhouette.

"I don't even know where this place is, Zoey. Underground we think, but who knows?"

"I don't know either. I was unconscious when they brought me in. I only remember waking up in this cell."

"It's too dangerous."

"We have to do something, Kim. We outnumber them. We could overtake them."

Kim shook her head; Zoey felt the rush of movement.

"But we have nothing to lose. It just keeps getting worse. I don't believe for a second that they'll let us go, either. Not after all of this. Not after what they did to Lucy."

Kim squeezed Zoey's hands. "If you try to escape, you'll be punished. I can't even imagine what they'd do. Besides, most of us are just too weak. And I've got some really nasty injuries."

"Yeah." She nodded. "I can barely walk."

"They can clean us up and give us ointments, but they never give us a chance to heal."

"I wonder how Lucy's doing?" Zoey said, pressing her forehead into the metal.

"I don't know." Kim sighed. "Don't know where she is. They didn't bring her back. I don't even know if she's still alive."

"All the more reason to get out of here, Kim. Are you in or not?"

Kim exhaled, her warm breath tickling Zoey's cheek. "I can't. I'll be getting out of here soon."

"You will?"

"Yes. James said I can probably go in a couple of weeks. I've been here almost eight months already."

Strings of hair fell in her eyes, and Zoey pushed them back. "Do you know the way out? I've been in most of the rooms but haven't seen an exit."

"In all the time I've been here, I've never see one. I've never seen any of the guards come or go. Listen, Zoey, I won't go with you, but maybe some of the others will. Ask around."

#

She'd been watching, trying to see where her tormentors went after they left the rooms, to see where they turned off as they wandered down the corridor. So hard to tell. Unmarked doors, and the guards never announced their departure or their destination, even to each other.

If she'd managed to keep track properly, which was almost impossible in their bizarre time-keeping methods, not knowing day from night, she guessed she'd been there at least a month.

Everyone was assembled in Room Five, large enough to hold all the prisoners (*guests*) and guards. Lucy still hadn't reappeared, and she'd been replaced by a new prisoner (*guest*).

Three women were chained naked, facing the wall, at the far end of the room.

James faced the audience. "Many of you have become lax. You seem to believe I'm kidding around. Perhaps you think that because you've been here a while, I won't go as hard on you as I would a newcomer. Not so, ladies, not so. As a matter of fact, since you already know the rules, I'm inclined to be even tougher on you.

"But I digress. What we have before us are three Guests who have forgotten the rules. Three who believed, perhaps, that this has become some sort of joke."

The woman closest to James slumped forward, her shoulders hitching.

James pulled on a pair of utility gloves and accepted a *cat o' nine tails*—thick reinforced shaft, multiple leather strands—from the guard Tony. Raised his arm, the whip overhead and behind his back, and struck the first women, then another, until he was whipping all three, each blow causing horrible screams. The *cat o' nine tails* split their flesh, left bloody welts exuding pus and gore on their backs and arms and legs, ample flesh quivering with each blow.

Breathing hard, hands on his knees, face glowing with exertion and happiness, James pointed at the first woman. "Sandra here spoke. Sandra's been here way too long to have made such a careless mistake." *Crack*! Sandra screamed, her body shaking, as if trying to break free of the chains.

He approached the middle woman. "Marie was late. Again." *Crack*! Flesh blood tricked down Marie's thigh, and she shuddered. "Mary's *always* late. Think now maybe she'll be on time?"

Crack! The third woman shrieked, threw back her head, falling toward her knees but caught by her wrists in the shackles. "Joanna . . . " James shook his head. "Joanna thought it was a good idea to attack a guard. There's no excuse for such an indiscretion. No forgiveness."

To the guard beside him he said, "Turn her around. And get me the ripper."

Joanna was unchained and she slumped against the guards who re-secured her to the wall, leaving her facing out.

Another guard handed James the ripper device. Four-pronged, like sets of fangs, two metal curved spikes jutting up from the bottom, two reaching down from the top.

Face already drenched with tears, Joanna sobbed harder.

"*No* forgiveness for assaulting a guard. No redemption. When one bites the hand that feeds her, the punishment must be severe. Some rules are never to be broken, such transgressions are intolerable. Let this be a lesson to all of you."

Gently, he raked the tool along her abdomen, pink streaks in its stead.

Joanna moaned, exhaling pent-up breath, her body trembling.

With a quick stroke he lifted the torture device up to her breast and tore through the fatty tissue, delicate skin bursting, white globules hanging, dripping from the destroyed breast.

Joanna's screams were shrill, hysterical, and James yanked the device up from the bottom of her torn body part, severing the breast from her body. It plopped on the floor, a gory lump of ru-ined tissue and desiccated milk ducts.

The smell of blood, coppery and salty, swam in her nostrils. Zoey retched into her palm.

James snapped his head back, fire blazing from his nostrils. "Anyone pukes, they fucking eat it!"

Handing the ripper and his heavy utility gloves to Tony, James said, "Get them out of here. Clean them up and put them in the cells."

James faced the prisoners. "Any questions?"

No one had any questions.

#

Everyone had been told to report to Room Twelve.

The pace in the corridor was rushed. No one wanted to risk being late, to have the flesh torn from her body . . . As much as she dreaded whatever waited for her in Room Twelve, Zoey hurried to get there.

She followed the crowd as they gathered outside the door. All of the prisoners were there—fifteen now, the three who had been punished now missing—and were told to form a line. One by one they were weighed. Zoey had lost twenty-six pounds.

She was told to go inside.

"Hey, Zoey." The young guard took her hand, led her to an area of the floor covered with mats. "You're supposed to have fun today, and I'll be helping you along."

He was upbeat, chipper, a goddamned boy scout. "My name's Kevin."

Yeah? Who the hell cares? The frustration felt when she'd made the decision to give up was almost as painful as the idea of the resignation itself. If Zoey had felt anguish at her inability to fight back before, it had become worse, since she was *unable* to fight, unable to save herself, unable to allow herself basic assumed rights.

Seeing the torture they were capable of inflicting drained her energy and her resolve . . . and Zoey decided to do as they demanded. Maybe things would get better somehow . . . maybe this would keep her whole, prevent them from shredding parts of her body away with a medieval torture device.

She slumped against the wall, eyes buried in the back of her wrist, and sobbed. Waited for the inescapable beating, the whipstrokes across her back, the tearing metal hooks rending her flesh into unrecognizable pulp.

Body shaking with her sobs, she couldn't stop. Weeks of frustration and pain washed away with the tears, acid rain that somehow was cleansing.

"Come with me," Kevin whispered in her ear, and led her away, her vision blurred, her eyes sore and puffy. She prayed that her punishment wouldn't be too severe, that she would survive it, and that it would end quickly.

Kevin brought her to a locked door behind the bathroom, a room off-limits to the prisoners. Inside was a sauna whirlpool, which smelled of chlorine and salts.

"The guards use it. It's . . . " He smiled, shrugged. "Relaxing." He led her up the few short steps to the edge of the pool. She stared at the steaming water, wondering if she was about to be boiled alive.

Kevin stripped, tossing his clothes and weapon in a pile by the door.

Zoey stood motionless at the top of the steps, arms crossed over her breasts. Approaching from behind, he moved her arms, gently pulled the shirt over her head and tossed it with his own clothes.

Leaned into her, pressed his lips into the back of her head. His fingertips traced her arms, moved further to caress her ribcage, her abdomen.

Tenderly he lay kisses on hr shoulders, trailed his tongue

along the musky, sweaty perfume of her skin. Lifted her hands over her head and stretched her body taut, and starting at her elbows followed her silhouette with butterfly kisses and pretend touches.

He motioned her forward and they stepped into the bubbling water, and like a thousand lovers' touches the water stimulated her legs, her pelvis.

Kevin turned her and they faced, and he took a nipple between his lips and held it in his mouth, his breath as steamy as the water. Took it between his teeth and she felt it harden. He grasped her buttocks and pulled her closer, rubbing his groin over hers, his stiffening cock probing, searching areas, as if waiting for her to receive him.

His mouth roamed from breast to collarbone to neck, licked her chin, discovered her lips.

But he pulled away, moved his cock so that it rested against her thigh. She wanted to touch it, wanted to feel it inside her, had not felt that way since she'd been brought to that wretched place. But something was different now. She needed the closeness, the tenderness of the man's touch. Needed the comfort of its delicate strength. Ached to feel it inside her, the velvety softness, the feeling of fullness, of *wanting*.

His fingertips barely dusted the surface of her skin, the endless length of organ alive and screaming and waiting for further touches, waiting for him to complete her.

With cupped palms he poured water over her hair, and carefully washed away dried blood and semen from her body.

She reached down and took his cock in her hand, but he pulled away, took her hands instead and laced his fingers into hers, bent his head and again found her lips. The water washed over them as they went down to their knees and rested, eyes closed, at the edge of the pool, the only sounds the light humming of the heater and the water lapping at the pool's edge.

"Feel better?" he whispered, breaking the magic spell, bringing her back to reality, but she nodded, held him tighter. His tongue probed between her lips and darted against her tongue.

A short while later he smiled. "Come on then," he said, leading her out of the pool.

They returned to the room where they had started. Zoey was strangely relaxed, and felt close to Kevin, felt as if she could trust him. It might have been a blind need to trust someone, anyone—she didn't know. But whatever the reason, his touches had been salvation, his manner a respite in the non-stop horror that had become her life.

All around them, couples were locked in embraces, some just starting, others fucking, twosomes and threesomes, a few foursomes.

Another man came over and knelt beside Zoey and Kevin. "Hey, can I play?" He smiled. Zoey felt that comfort zone quickly dissolving.

Kevin took Zoey's hand in his. "Zoey, this is Todd. Okay if he joins us?"

She wondered why he had even bothered to ask. As if she had a real choice. She shrugged.

"Trust me," Kevin said.

"I guess I have good timing," Todd said. "What were you about to do?" His fingers traced the edge of Zoey's shoulders, barely-there strokes. "How about if I start down here?"

Kevin gently pushed Zoey on her back. Todd bent her legs, spread them. Gently slipped his fingers between her labia and pushed them inside her. Rosebuds bloomed on her cheeks, and her breath caught in her throat, surprised by the tenderness of his touch. Muscles tensed, expecting the pain that seemed inescapable.

"She's really tight," Todd said. "Loosen her up."

Kevin cupped her breast, rolled the nipple between his fingers. He kissed her, fervent breath on her cheek, her lips, his tongue filling her mouth. He guided her hand to his rock-hard erection, glistening with pre-cum.

Todd spread her wide with his thumbs, exposing her hyper-sensitive clit. Nerve endings sparked wildly, filling her with intense pleasure.

The contradiction of feelings tore her apart. She despised this place, despised what they had done to her, but this . . . this felt good. Accepting this, allowing herself to *feel*, was something she had a difficult time accepting.

Kevin moved in closer, lifted his engorged shaft to her mouth, tried to guide it between her lips. At first she refused, turned her head, but then turned back to him. Propped herself up on her elbow. He slid his turgid cock inside her mouth. She sucked, licked the shaft, wrapped her mouth around his ball sack.

Todd had gotten her wet, incredibly wet, warm juices puddling between her legs, and he eased himself into her.

They pulled out, guided her to her hands and knees, and Todd slipped in from behind. Kevin guided himself into her mouth and she accepted him.

"Are you cumming?" Todd cried shortly after, strokes increasing, and she moaned, so damned close now, breath fast and furious, a tidal wave of pleasure. She'd cum before, even when being raped, but she'd despised it, had felt torn about experiencing anything enjoyable, about feeling anything at all when she'd been so brutally fucked.

But now—now she was allowing herself happiness, accepting the inevitability. Her brain had shut down and all that remained was primal heat, the need to feel closeness, a gentle touch.

Todd came and she groaned, her shuddery orgasm intense and powerful, her legs trembling on wave after wave of ecstasy. Kevin exploded inside her mouth, groaned in blissful agony.

The three lay tangled in a sweaty heap, chests rapidly rising and falling, the heady scent of spent sex in the air.

The respite didn't last long. She was passed from group to

group, enmeshed in the orgy, accepting her fate in the room, knowing it might never be this good again in this awful place.

Somehow, it had become bearable. Somehow she'd *made it* bearable. Praying for death was easy, but she had chosen to fight for life instead, a new way of life, a way that she had slowly been forced to accept.

Hours later she returned to her cell, aching, exhausted, semen leaking out of her cunt like a bad infection. The sheet provided little warmth or protection but it felt good against her skin, felt familiar, like home.

Chapter 9

Sunshine on her face, warm, gleaming, and smells of flesh gently baking, of wildflower perfume.

She tasted the heat on her tongue, felt it on her skin. Opened her eyes to the brilliance of the sun spotlighting the endless meadow, tall grasses bowing, poppies dancing, a rush of movement when the wind picked up. Splashes of color, a backdrop for the trees and underbrush.

Laying on her cot, eyes pinched tightly shut, Zoey woke but tried to stay lost in the dream. Remembering summers in the country, afternoons at the lake, of dipping her toes in the chilled mountain water in the brook behind their house. Playing tag with her sister and the neighborhood kids. Mother cat in the barn loft, birthing six kittens.

If she opened her eyes now, the image would be lost. It had already begun to falter. The afternoon sun faded behind her eyes until it was nothing but a blackened smudge. Zoey stared at her eyelids and tried to retrieve a dream that had died a slow and painful death.

Opened her eyes, knew they were open because she felt her lashes dust the tops of her cheekbones, but she saw nothing. No windows to sneak in dribbles of sunlight, no overhead or wall lights to create shadows in the corners of the cell. No way to know the time, to know to try to go back to sleep, or stay awake. Perpetual nothingness in a stygian blackness.

"Anyone else up?" she whispered.

"Yeah. I am. Janice."

"Do you think it's time to get up?"

"I have no idea. Try to sleep."

Zoey nodded, which answered no one.

"I'm awake, too," said another voice. "Heather."

"Marie? Are you awake?" Zoey was worried about her, and the other women who had been severely beaten with the cat o' nine tails. "Marie?"

"I'm here," she said, sounding tired, in pain.

"Are you okay?" Zoey asked.

"Not really. Can't lay on my back. They bandaged me up, but it still burns."

"Me too," Sandra said. "This was a bad one. Bastard. I swear to god I'm going to kill him one of these days."

"Hey—you all know what today is?" Janice asked. When no one responded, she said, "I've been counting off the days. We're having company."

"Oh, shit no," Heather gasped. "Are you sure?"

"Yeah. Pretty sure. They always do this right after their little orgy."

"What are you talking about?" Zoey asked.

There was silence, as if no one wanted to talk about it.

Another voice spoke up, and this one Zoey recognized as Kim. "They bring in people from the outside, to watch. And . . . other stuff."

"People? What people?" Zoey felt a ray of hope. Maybe one of these people would help. Maybe—

"A group of goddamned perverts, that's what they are," Sandra said.

The hope exploded in Zoey's chest. "What do they do?"

"Anything they want," Heather said. "They pay good money

for it."

"You sure that's today?" Zoey cried. "Maybe you're wrong."

"Once every other month. The first Saturday. And unless I've been counting wrong, today's Saturday." Janice sounded almost excited.

"God, Janice, it sounds horrible," Zoey said, sinking into her pillow, wishing she'd never asked. Wiggled her fingers in front of her face. Nothing.

A short while later, the bolt was thrown, the main door opened. Overhead lights blared into life.

"Rise and shine," the guard, Matthew said. Moments later the buzzer sounded, unlocking the cells.

Adjusting to the harsh light was painful, and Zoey squinted, her lids fluttering.

In a single line they headed toward the bathroom to shower, to wash away the dirt and sweat from the day before, to clean dried cum and crusted blood from their bodies. They weren't allowed to shower at night and were forced to sleep in the filth and body fluids that clung to their bodies like second skin.

Guards watched them shower.

"Do a good job now," Tony said. "We're having Visitors."

They were handed clean towels and T-shirts as they left the shower area.

At breakfast, Zoey pushed her food around on the plate and was experiencing a new breed of anxiety.

"Is it bad?" she whispered to Kim, sitting beside her. "These people?"

Kim nodded. "Sometimes. Depends on who you get." Eggs spilled off her fork. "Or how many."

The eggs suddenly looked revolting, quivering mounds of embryo.

Something else had been bothering her. "Kim . . . I should have had my period by now. Do you think I might be . . . ?"

"No, and you won't get your period. They put birth control in the food."

Eyebrows raised. "What?" She glanced down at the food. "But sometimes I skip a meal. What if—"

"They put it in all the food, at every meal. The chance of getting pregnant is nearly impossible."

"Oh, comforting."

Janice sat across from them, dropping her tray on the table in disgust. "Good morning. My, don't you all look sparkling clean?"

Kim smiled. "Special day. We even get the good soap."

"Eat up, Zoey," Janice said. "You'll need your strength."

She shook her head. "I can't. It's making me nauseous." The coffee went down okay, but she refused to put those eggs near her mouth. "Janice, how long have you been here?"

"Five months, more or less. I was pretty big when they brought me in here."

"I guess you must have been," Zoey said, pushing her tray to the center of the table. "You're thin now."

"Almost. A few more pounds."

Zoey planted her face in her palms, and rested her elbows on the table. "What do you suppose happens?"

"When?" Janice chewed on a piece of bacon and pushed her too-long blonde hair off her face.

"You know, after you're done. After you—"

"When you lose the weight? They let you go."

Zoey stared at Janice. "They let you go? Just like that?"

"That's what they say," Kim said, shrugging.

Zoey said, "But why would they?"

"Because no one talks. Because this is far-reaching, Zoey." Janice picked up her toast, took a bite. "You don't know what goes on outside this place."

"How do you know?" Zoey asked.

Janice shrugged. "Like I said, I've been here a while. I hear things. The guards say things, other subjects who have been here a long time."

"Subjects?"

"She means prisoners, Zoey," Kim said. "Janice has a unique perspective."

Janice used her toast like an extended finger and pointed across the room. "See that guard by the door? That's Robin. She used to be a subject."

Zoey's jaw dropped. Robin was the one who had brutalized her with a nightstick. "My god . . . you're kidding. They made her stay?" She wondered how a former prisoner could perpetuate the torture.

Janice laughed, spraying crumbs across the table. "Not at all. She chose the job."

Robin leaned against the door, arms crossed over her chest. She yawned.

Zoey looked back at the women at the table. "She chose it? Why?"

"Not everyone here hates it, Zoey. Some of us actually enjoy it. Usually." Janice grinned, forked eggs into her mouth.

Zoey glanced at Kim. "What about you?"

"What about me? I'm just killing time. I'm anxious to leave. Unlike Janice here."

Janice licked her lips, wiped her mouth on the back of her hand. "What can I say? I like to fuck. This place is like Nirvana for me. At first I hated it, being forced to do this stuff. But then I decided to pretend it was my choice. I got into it, you know? After a while it got better. And now . . . well, now I just go out there and enjoy myself."

"You're seriously disturbed, Janice." Zoey shook her head, dropped her napkin on the plate. "What I want to know is how these guys get it up every time, over and over . . . It's not natural."

"They're juiced up. They take stuff to keep them hard. Viagra I guess, other stuff." Janice smiled and glanced across the room.

James had entered, and all conversations stopped as if severed with a knife.

"Good morning," he said. "I'm sure you all know by now that today is Visiting Day. For those of you who don't know what that is, let's just say it's a chance for you to get acquainted with some new blood. I expect you all to be on your best behavior."

He looked from woman to woman, as if inspecting them. Haunted faces stared back. "Let me make one thing clear. These people are not here to rescue you. They know you're not volunteers. *They don't care.* Understand? If I hear that any of you asked for help, you won't be able to walk for a month.

"You will do whatever they tell you. Some will only want to watch, but there aren't many who don't want to be hands-on. So to speak." Stuck out his tongue, tittered at his little joke." Breakfast is over. Get your assignments."

#

Zoey stood outside Room Eleven, fingers trailing the chipping paint. Chewed a loose bit of skin on her lip, filled her lungs. Entered the room.

A playpen in the corner, large enough to hold a dozen sleeping children. Full size rocking chair beside it. A banquet table in the center of the small room, covered with sheets; bottles of lotion, creams, baby powder were assembled near the edge. Mobiles of toy boats and grinning clowns hung from the ceiling, danced in the air conditioned breeze.

Someone cleared his throat, and Zoey spun around. Four men, including the guard, Kevin, stood hidden in the shadows.

A man stepped forward, ample flesh covering his tall frame. He wore a diaper and nothing else.

Zoey took a half step back.

"Go ahead, Serge," Kevin said. "You've done this before. Tell her what you want."

Serge waddled toward her, belly and jowls jiggling. "Take off your clothes."

She pulled off the T-shirt and dropped it on the floor. The room was colder than the others, and her nipples hardened.

Serge smiled, licked his lips. "Nice. Nice one, Kevin." He took Zoey's hand and led her into the nursery. Lowered her to her knees and followed her to the floor, and lay his head in her lap.

Kevin. Why did Kevin have to be here?

"Lean down." Serge pulled her closer. Reached up, fondled a breast. "Lower."

Her chest was over his face, and he guided a breast into his mouth and sucked. The other breast he yanked, rough then gentle then rough.

Kevin had stepped out of the shadows, was standing outside the nursery area. "Serge is your baby, Zoey. He's hungry. Make sure he gets plenty of milk."

She rolled her eyes, groaned. Any hope she might have felt walking into the room, any thought of recruiting their help, slowly dissolved until it faded into nothing.

Serge sucked harder, pulled it into his throat, slid it in and out of his mouth, lightly chewed on the nipple, made suckling noises. The other he held in a savage vise-like grip, twisting the nipple.

He switched breasts, now tasting the one he had abused. Spasms of pain, tiny needle gashes inflicted by barracuda teeth. He guided her hand to his swollen phallus, and she wanted nothing more than to rip it off his body.

He released her breast, roamed until it found her pubis, stroked the short, curly hair. He hooked a finger into the top of her vagina and yanked her toward him. She gasped, lifted her groin, and he pushed his fingers inside her, rubbed his thumb over the clit.

He pulled her breast out of his mouth. "Now do me."

She looked up at Kevin. Had no idea what he wanted.

"He wants you to suck his breasts, Zoey," Kevin said, establishing eye contact with her, and he mouthed *I'm sorry*, and shook his head.

Ragged breaths. Pulled her hair back and leaned into him, twisted his nipple with her lips, tiny hairs embedded in her teeth. She imagined herself chewing it right off his body and spitting it back in his ugly, hairy face.

"Oh, yes . . . " he groaned. "I feel it . . . it's coming . . . " His face scrunched, as if in pain, and then he smiled. A sudden putrid odor filled the room. She retched, covering her mouth with her hand.

Serge sat up, pushed himself to his knees. Took her hand and together they stood. "Come. You have to clean me now."

"Wha—"

He led her to the banquet table and climbed on, lying on his back.

Oh no. The smell was stronger now, and it was coming from Serge. She looked at Kevin, her eyes begging, body filled with a pervasive dread at what she was expected to do. This was impossible. How could they expect her to do this?

Kevin dropped his gaze to the floor. "You know what he wants, Zoey. The diapers are on the floor in the bag there." Adult disposable diapers.

Oh good god, no . . . Wanted to scream, frantically searched for a way out of this one.

Serge kicked his feet and snatched her breast, pulling hard, ruthlessly. "Do it!" he snapped.

It was almost impossible to control her trembling hands. She grabbed a diaper from the bag, lay it on the table. Pulled the powder and lotion closer.

Serge closed his eyes, shook his shoulders as if snuggling into the table. The diaper on his body was secured with Velcro tabs, and she undid them, pulled the front of the diaper down over his crotch, revealing his engorged penis. And the load of shit in the diaper.

She gagged, covered her mouth with her arm. Her eyes watered. She snatched the roll of paper towels, yanked off a pile of sheets.

There was no way to pretend this one away. No way to imagine old boyfriends, or anything that might help her get through this. She just had to finish as quickly as possible.

"You fucking bastard!" she screamed, pounding his face, pulling the diaper out from under him and mashing the shit in his face. Grabbed his testicles and pulled, squeezed, rupturing them, twisted until they popped, until—

"Zoey?" Kevin said. "Hurry up."

It felt good while it lasted, her little fantasy. She turned her head away, held her breath. Reached in with the paper towels and wiped the shit off his ass, wrapped it in the dirty diaper and rolled it up, pushing it to the end of the table. Grabbed a moist cloth and wiped him clean, applied lotion and baby powder. Picked up the clean diaper and spread it.

Cum dribbled out of his dick. He grabbed it, gave it a couple of strokes. "Come here, Zoey." He patted the table.

She bit her tongue, climbed up and knelt beside him. He slid over until he was centered.

"Sit on my face."

Slowly she climbed his torso until her crotch straddled his face. Refused to allow the tears to fall, wouldn't give them the satisfaction of seeing her distress.

Lowered herself, felt his gaseous breath, felt his lips inside her, getting her wet, his head bobbing, following the movement of his tongue. His fingers played with her from behind, caressed her ass, probed her anus.

He pushed her away. "Fuck me, Zoey! Fuck me good."

She climbed back down his body until she found his cock. Straddled it, lowered herself onto it, thighs trembling. Rode him like the horse that he was, a snorting, foaming beast, his face flushed red with excitement and exertion.

"Harder! Fuck me!"

She pumped harder, faster, sliding up and down on his stiff member until he shuddered, moaned loudly, embalmed her with hot, sticky fluid, gripped the sheet.

Legs aching, she climbed off. She looked up. The other men stood at the head of the table. Once wore a diaper, the other was naked, his diaper in his hand.

The naked one motioned for her to climb down, and he took her wrist and lowered her to the floor, pushed her onto her back. He held his flaccid penis in his hand and hovered over her. She was expecting him to put it in her mouth.

She wasn't expecting what he did.

Urine shot out, splashed her breasts. He controlled the stream, directed it up and down her body.

Shocked, she sucked in a quick breath, then shut her mouth and turned her head to avoid getting splashed in the face. Strong stink of ammonia filled her nostrils, permeated the room. He pissed in her hair.

When he finished she looked back, stunned, piss dripping off her head. He shook out the final drops.

"Thank you," he said, grinning. "That's all I wanted. I prefer to watch." He sat in the rocking chair, crossed his legs, his cock dangling between them.

Arms thrown back, she raised her head toward the ceiling and screamed. Couldn't stop. Her body shook, chest heaved. Piss tricked down her forehead and stung her eyes.

The Visitors laughed.

"Oooh, she's been bad," Serge said. "She needs to be punished."

Fuck! she thought, wanting to scream again. Wanting to kill them all.

"What do you want to do about it, Frank?" Serge asked.

"I know exactly what I want to do." Frank moved to the foot of the changing table and dragged out a satchel. Pulled out a strap.

"Come here, Zoey," he said, patting the table.

Her legs were weak, could barely support her. Urine dried on her body, chilling her. She approached Frank, climbed up as he instructed. Face down, on her stomach. She expected the strikes to be soft at first, then increase in severity, the way they normally did things around here.

Frank surprised her. The first strike was powerful, sharp and painful, each blow that followed equally harsh. She screamed and cried, held her hands behind her back. Serge grabbed them, pulled them above her head, flat on the table.

Raw, smoldering heat, a swarm of hornets relentlessly stinging her back, her ass, the backs of her legs.

She heard Kevin approach, and the beating stopped. Her flesh was a pit of hellfire. "That's enough, gentlemen," he said softly. "I think she—"

"Get the fuck out of here, pipsqueak," Serge said. Zoey tilted her head, saw Serge shove Kevin's chest, knocking the much smaller man back a few steps.

The other two laughed.

"What else you got in that bag of tricks?" Frank asked.

Zoey tried to kneel but an enormous hand pushed her down, slapped her tender ass. "Stay put, sweet cheeks," Serge said.

"Gentlemen," Kevin said, approaching the table again. "This isn't part of the agreement. The rules—"

"Fuck the rules, tiny," Serge said. "You wanna get lost, or you wanna take her place?"

"Hey, look what I found," Frank said. Zoey felt his hands on her legs, on her ass. "Get on your knees."

She hesitated, and he smacked her. "Move! Spread your legs."

On her hands and knees. He pushed something inside her, something that felt like a penis, but she knew from painful experience that it was a dildo.

"Guys, please!" Kevin cried. "Don't do this. I've asked you to stop."

Zoey looked up in time to see Serge rush Kevin, punch him in the face. Kevin went down like a sack of laundry.

Wet fingers penetrated her anus, moved around inside her.

She grunted, arms and legs quaking, sweat popping out on her forehead despite the chilled air. The fingers slipped out, were replaced by yet another dildo. Sphincter muscles clenched, tried uselessly to force it out.

The two dildos filled her, the pain maddening. Her insides were raw, felt shredded. A wave of nausea struck, and she felt weaker still.

"Can you reach from there?" Serge asked.

"Yeah, I think so," Frank said. "Why don't you have her lean forward?"

Serge pushed Zoey's back until her chest rested on the table, her hind quarters still sticking up.

"Hey, Jeff—you want in?" Frank asked.

"No, thank you. I enjoy watching."

Without warning Frank slapped her with the belt, a direct hit on the dildo protruding from her ass, pushing it further in. Her stomach flipped, bile clawed its way up her throat.

She wailed, tried to move away. Serge leaned on her shoulders, his enormous upper body smothering her, holding her in place. "Don't fucking move, bitch."

Another strike on her ass, and another, repeating the blows until she thought she was going to die from the agony. A blast of color danced in the air before her eyes.

The assault stopped.

"Turn her over," Frank said, short hard gasps.

Serge flipped her on her back. They spread her legs wide, both ankles hanging over opposite sides of the table.

"No good," Frank said. "Here—try this." Took her ankles, legs still spread, lifted them toward the ceiling.

Serge grinned, his jowls jiggling. His back now to Zoey's face, he took her legs and pulled them back, until they were almost at a ninety degree angle to the rest of her body.

"Hold them wide," Frank said. "And move your head, man. I don't want to get you by mistake."

Serge leaned back, his fingers a vise-grip on her ankles, his elbows pressed painfully against her chest.

The assault started again. Frank beat her with the belt, each strike smashing one dildo into the other, stripping the tender flesh of her vaginal walls.

Beyond screams, she groaned, rolled her head, eyelids fluttering, trying desperately to remain conscious. Blow after blow, relentless, the blood draining from her head.

Frank stopped, wiped his forehead with the back of his hand. "Hey—where'd that little pipsqueak go?"

"He crawled out of here a few minutes ago," Jeff said from the rocking chair.

Zoey shivered, praying for help from a god that had long-since forsaken her. Hoping Kevin would hurry back and end this torment. Closed her eyes and waited for relief, either from rescue or death.

"He's in for a surprise," Serge said, and they all laughed.

Frank smiled. "Sure is. Hey—we done with this one?"

"Guess so," Serge said, dropping her legs.

"You want a turn?" Frank asked Serge.

"No, later. I got a raging boner though. Clear out her pussy."

Frank pulled out the dildo and a stream of blood followed. "Kind of messy in there."

"Yeah, so?" Serge knelt on the table, straddled her, stroked his cock. Bent her knees, fucked her.

Searing heat. She thought she'd felt more pain than she could handle by now, but she'd been wrong. She got to experience it all over again. Eyes clamped shut, couldn't watch, unable to react any more, screams and tears wasted effort.

He pulled out just before ejaculating. Stroked himself and jacked off on her stomach. Slapped his penis against her thigh.

"What is this?" Frank laughed. "A fucking porn movie?"

Serge huffed. "Take her with us?"

Frank said. "I don't feel like dragging her around. We'll come back for her. She's not going anywhere."

They left.

She didn't move for a long time. The tears streamed into her hair. When she tried to move her legs the pain worsened. With a trembling hand she reached behind and pulled the dildo out of her ass. Blood gushed, soaked the sheet. Slowly she turned on her side, her stomach churning with cramps, and curled into a ball. Pulled the blood-soaked sheet over her body.

The clock above the door loudly ticked off the seconds, and the air conditioner's hum droned on, the only other sounds in the room besides her gentle weeping.

More time passed and still no one returned. She located a clean corner of the sheet and pressed it between her legs, trying to absorb the trickling fluids. She sat up, her body fighting the movement.

Still no one came.

Using the table for support, she lowered her legs to the floor. They buckled, rebelled against supporting her. She waited for the shakes to stop and stood up. With agonizing slowness she made her way across the room, stopping only to retrieve her T-shirt and pull it on over her head. Wrapped the sheet around her waist.

She had to leave but was afraid to. Would they be angry? Was she supposed to wait there, bleeding to death? Would James punish her for breaking yet another *rule*? This had never happened before. Everything was always so orderly, so calculated, run a specific way. The prisoners (Guests) were always given instructions before being allowed to leave a room. So now what? Would she be punished for leaving?

Bathroom, had to get to the bathroom. She crept into the hall, expecting the usual busyness, but the corridor was empty. No guards stationed, no prisoners rushing to their next assignments.

She leaned against the wall for support, smearing bloody fingerprints. Gore trickled down her thighs. She fashioned the sheet like a diaper.

No sound. Voices were nonexistent. On her left, the bathroom was about six doors down. She headed in that direction. Room after room was dark, appeared deserted.

A bit further down was the cafeteria. Zoey approached, planning to head back to the bathroom. The door was open a crack, and Zoey discovered where everyone was.

Chapter 10

Zoey's heart slammed in her chest as she leaned in closer to the door, open wide enough for her to hear what was going on inside. Something felt terribly wrong, and instinct told her to stay away. But she had to know what was happening.

At first she heard laughter, a loud bellow.

"Fuck you!" James yelled. Zoey peered in through the small slit separating the doors.

"No, James. Fuck *you*."

She didn't recognize the man who had James by the hair, the man who then punched James in his stomach and dropped him to the floor.

At the head of the room stood the three Visitors who had tortured her. Beside them stood three other men.

"My name is Zachary," the man who had punched James said to the roomful of prisoners and guards—all prisoners now, it seemed. "Call me Zack." He smiled, crossed his arms over his black T-shirt. "In case you haven't guessed, James is no longer in charge. Neither are his asshole cohorts. From now on, you'll all do as *I* say."

Shifted his feet, ran his hand over his black hair. "We're going to have fun, ladies. And gentlemen. Just do as you're told, and we'll all get along just great. No one will get hurt. Wait, scratch that. Just do as you're told."

He paced, slow steps across the front of the room. "We got sick of the way things have been run around here. Got sick of this once every other month bullshit. We pay way too goddamn much money. And we thought our way would be more fun. Don't you agree?"

Fun? Was that what they considered fun? She glanced over her shoulder at the empty hallway, turned her attention back to the cafeteria.

Zack faced the women who stared back at him in stunned silence. He smashed his fist into a table. "Answer me!"

Women shouted or mumbled "yes!".

"Better." He turned to the other Visitors. "Everyone accounted for?"

"I left some in the medieval room," a man dressed in a monk's robe said. "They're chained up, though."

"We left one in the nursery," Serge said. Then he grinned, added, "She's not going anywhere."

"Pete, Doug, go get them, drag their sorry asses in here. Serge—room number?"

Serge shrugged. "How should I know? It's the nursery."

"Wally? Room number?"

The monk shook his head. "I didn't notice, Zack."

"Oh for fuck's sake, somebody tell me the room numbers."

Zoey stepped away from the door, walked backwards down the hall. Shaking hands guided her way along the wall. She needed to hide—but where? Her mind searched every room, but there was no time to think. A few more feet down the hall, she ducked into the bathroom. Killed the lights, and left the door ajar so she could hear them approaching.

The toilet stalls had no doors. The shower area was a large, open room with overhead jets. No place to hide in there either. The linen closet was located at the back of the bathroom, behind the showers, and she rushed toward it. The darkness prevented her from seeing, but she knew what the closet looked like, lined with shelves, loaded with towels and T-shirts.

Working quickly, she removed half the contents of one shelf onto the others, rearranging them to look as natural as possible, guided only by blind instinct. She stuffed herself into the narrow shelf, hiding behind stacks of towels and shirts, pulled the door shut and drew them toward her, desperately hoping she hadn't knocked any to the floor. It was impossible to know in the caliginous room. Her already pain-wracked body ached even more from being stuffed into the small space. Under other circumstances, there was no way she would have imagined fitting inside that closet.

She didn't know what she was going to do. They were probably already looking for her, and when they discovered she was gone from the nursery, they would likely tear the place apart looking. Surrender was an option—maybe they would go easy on her if she did. But then, she thought, if they'd beaten her so badly in fun, what the hell would they do to her in anger?

No, better to hide, to think.

She managed to turn onto her back, legs spread, the damaged flesh between her thighs screaming, but it relieved the stress on her contorted limbs.

No way to know how long she lay there, in the dark, cramped space, waiting to be discovered. But after a while the voices came, angry and frustrated, slamming doors.

From the closeness of the voices, she knew.

They were inside the bathroom.

Chapter 11

The darkness was feral, powerful, tried to suck the oxygen out of her lungs. She gasped, then held her breath. Terror gripped her bowels and squeezed.

Furious voices, closer now.

The overpowering smell of bleach burned her nostrils, coated her tongue with a metallic and cold tang.

"No doors." And unfamiliar male voice. "No doors in this fucking bathroom!"

"Then where the hell is she?"

"The fuck should I know? Let's split. She's gotta be hiding in one of the rooms."

The voices trailed off.

They hadn't found the linen closet. Yet.

She relaxed for a second, exhaled.

The door to the closet was thrown open. Tiny cracks of light filtered through the stacks of towels and shirts. Opened her mouth and nearly screamed, caught herself in time.

"Nothing, goddammit. Linens and shit." Same voice as before.

"She's not in there?"

"*Where*? The shelves are too small."

"Maybe we should empty it out."

"You wanna do all that work, be my guest. I came here to fuck, not to work. All we've been doing since we got here is work. This is bullshit, man."

"Yeah, I know." But he moved closer, seemed to be inspecting the contents of the shelf above her.

"Come on, let's go already." Seconds later, the bathroom door slammed.

This time they didn't come back.

The position in the closet had become unbearable, and her legs were screaming, knees numb. Wanted desperately to get out, but not yet, had to wait a little longer. Had to think. There had to be some other place to hide. Had to find the way out of the torture chamber. Couldn't escape to any of the rooms because they were probably using them. The cells? Nowhere to hide there either, and she didn't want to get trapped.

Kitchen? She'd never been in the kitchen and had no idea if there would be a place to hide. Probably a pantry or a freezer, but how would she be able to remain undetected in a freezer? Or remain alive in one, for that matter.

And she had the feeling that these men weren't planning on leaving any time too soon. She had the feeling that this was a new regime.

They were back. Peals of laughter, and what sounded like a scuffle. Snorts and groans, and a loud smacking thud, like someone hitting the floor.

"Stay there, asshole!"

Moments later the bathroom door slammed shut.

A low moan, from inside the room. *Oh, god, now what?*

"Fuckers . . . " someone said, but there was no strength in the voice. Zoey slid the stack of towels over a bit so she could hear better.

"Just wait," he said, words slurring, sounding wet, thick.

She recognized the voice. She pushed the towels aside and pushed open the closet door. Moving slowly, her joints cracking and protesting, she peeked out into the shower area.

James was staring up at her with his undamaged eye, a stunned expression on his face. "I'll be damned," he muttered, his grin revealing bloodied teeth. "Zoey."

Still wasn't sure she wanted to climb out. Was this a trap? A test? Had he somehow known she was hiding there?

She exited the closet feet first. Droplets of blood plinked to the floor, formed tiny circles and crowns.

James laughed, then doubled over and clutched his stomach, a phlegmy cough wracking him.

The tingling in her legs was fierce, a swarm of yellow jackets beneath her skin. Landing on her feet sent currents through her body.

"Aren't you resourceful?" he said, and she saw something new on his face: fear. Was he afraid of *her*? More likely he was afraid of the situation. Not that he didn't deserve to die a slow and agonizing death, and not that she hadn't fantasized torturing him to death. She outweighed him, and he was in sorry shape. Killing him now would be easy.

She sat next to him on the floor. "We're alone?"

He nodded.

"Care to explain, James?"

"I was about to ask you the same thing."

"Who are these pricks?"

"Clients. Disgruntled clients. Customers." Gingerly he touched his eye, badly swollen, dribbling pus. "These guys are our regulars. They come here to have some fun."

"Fun?" The desire to claw his face off returned. She glanced at the bathroom door, hoping she'd have time to hide if they came back.

"I'm sorry, Zoey. This got out of hand."

"You have a knack for understatement, James. How did this happen? You outnumber them. You got more guards than—"

"They have guns."

She hadn't seen guns. But it made sense. How else would they have been able to overpower James and his staff?

"This is really bad news," he said, gently wiping the blood off his cheek with his palm. "These guys are seriously disturbed."

"Oh, and you're not?"

"These guys make me look like a priest. Wait—bad example."

"I get the idea."

"Last time, Serge—the one with the diaper fetish —?"

"I know him well."

"Last time he was here, he approached me with the idea of making a snuff film. I thought he was kidding."

Zoey narrowed her eyes. "You thought he was kidding? Who jokes about that?"

"I know. But I told him no way. He said fine, he understood. I thought that was the end of it. These guys pay huge amounts of money to pay their visits. I usually look the other way when they want to try strange things. Besides, they're not exactly pillars of society. Zack's deeply involved in the drug scene, not the kind of guy you want to fuck with."

"Comforting. Do you have any idea whatsoever in that psycho fucked-up head of yours how wrong all of this is? Including your bizarre idea of a weight loss program?"

James shifted uncomfortably. "There have been studies, Zoey. Women who lose weight have said they're rather lose a limb than gain it back. This is an extreme weight loss plan."

"That seems to be your motto around here. You really are in-sane."

"No." He shook his head. "I'm not. I'm quite sane. But I *am* a sociopath." He smiled at that.

"I thought you said you were some filthy rich asshole with too much time on his hands."

"I am."

"Then why do you care about the money? About them paying you a fortune?"

"I don't. It was just a statement."

She rolled her eyes, turned away. "We're going to die. Aren't we?"

He thought for a moment. "Probably. The only thing we can hope for is a quick and painless one. Although I don't think there's much chance of that, especially for me."

"We have to do something."

"Really. Like what?"

"I don't know. Something."

She moved back and leaned against the wall, stretched her legs out in front of her. "They don't know about me. Where I am."

"Oh, they're searching for you."

"Still?"

"Of course. Ripping the place apart. They've begun their party games, though."

"How can I get out of this place?"

"You can't."

"There's a way out."

"Trust me, Zoey. There's no way out, except for the main exit, and that's heavily guarded, I'm sure. Especially with you missing. Besides, you can't even get out of the bathroom. They've locked the door."

Feeling had returned to her legs. "Where's the exit, James?"

He seemed preoccupied with the gash on his arm.

"Goddammit, James . . . " she muttered. "What do you think they're going to do with you?"

It was a long time before he answered. "I'm afraid to think about that."

Chapter 12

The harsh fluorescent lights aggravated her eyes, and every time she shifted, her body was reacquainted with pain. A full bladder caused even more discomfort, and she was afraid to relieve herself. Afraid of the pan, afraid of the noise she would make.

"I need to use the toilet," she said, shifting, looking up at James.

"Oh." He propped himself up on an elbow. "Can you do it quietly? You won't be able to flush or anything."

"I know. The problem is, they did some serious damage to me. I don't know what'll happen when I start to pee."

He chewed his lip. "What did they do to you?"

"They shoved dildos inside me and then beat me with a strap. Right before and after that fat fuck raped me."

He lowered his head, which surprised her. "Zoey, I'm sorry, I really am. It got out of hand, and . . . "

"Save it, James. You're sorry? You're a fucking hypocrite. You've been doing this shit to me for over a month."

Raising her voice hadn't been a good idea. Still, no movement at the door. At least it didn't seem like she had been too loud.

"But it's always controlled. We always stopped before we went too far."

"I've been fucked by a dog, James. And one of those sick assholes *pissed* on me. All part of the fun and games? You told us all to do exactly what they said. So don't try to justify your psychotic actions, James. You're no better than they are. You're just not running the show any more. You got exactly what you deserve."

Now she wondered if she'd gone too far, said too much. Would he call the men, turn her in?

"I don't know what to say, Zoey. I *am* sorry. Anything I've done was for control, order. No one was ever harmed who didn't deserve it."

"So if this ended right now, if you were to regain control, would you shut down your research facility?"

No response to that question.

The room spun as she struggled to her feet, using the wall for support as she clawed her way up. "I need to try to use the toilet."

Every white-hot step seared her internally. Her heart throbbed, and her mouth was dry.

"Need help, Zoey?"

"No." She hobbled to the stalls. At least there were stalls, even though there were no doors. What little privacy they offered was hardly much comfort.

She lifted her shirt and sat on the toilet. At first it refused to come, anxiety freezing her bladder, and she forced herself to relax.

The first drops almost made her scream. Torment again, red-hot pokers. Open wounds sizzled and pulsed, and she waited an eternity for her bladder to empty. The toilet paper she used was soaked with blood. She wadded up more and pushed it inside her like a tampon, trying to dry it. She pulled it out, and it was also soaked. Several applications later, she had it under control.

Supporting herself against the wall, she stood, nearly flushed out of habit. The water was sanguineous, mottled with blood clots. The exertion stole her breath, drained her small reserve of energy as she made her way outside the stall.

Voices outside the bathroom. Her head jerked from side to side, as if she had a decision to make, as if she had any options at all. The stall was all she had, and she moved back inside and straddled the toilet, moved as far back as she could. Trying to get back to the linen closet wasn't an option.

The lock was thrown, the bathroom door slammed open.

"Let's go, asshole." The voice drifted toward the showers, along with footsteps belonging to more than one person.

"Where?" James asked.

"Just get the fuck up. Zack wants you to join the party."

A soft thud, a grunt from James.

"Move!"

She heard them scuffling, then their footsteps were heading back toward her direction.

Pressed up against the wall, tried to melt into the plaster and paint. Squeezed her eyes but not completely shut, wanted to see them if they approached her.

The small procession stopped at the door, and she was sure they would find her, that maybe they could hear her raspy breath, could smell the fresh, bloody piss that stank like copper and rotten fish.

Instead, they left.

After several minutes—the longest minutes of her life—she peered outside the stall. The bathroom door was ajar.

She slumped against the wall.

Now what?

The same dilemma that had brought her to the bathroom to begin with returned. No place to hide.

There was another level to the torture chamber, that shrink's office. She recalled walking up a short flight of stairs, had thought before reaching his office that it had been the way out. Although she hadn't seen an exit. But still . . .

She stood behind the bathroom door and listened. Voices, but not close. Down the hall, around Room Four, a few doors away. Someone started to yell, a man's voice, and someone else started sobbing.

Slapping sounds. A woman screamed. Rushed footsteps, and the corridor was silent. A door slammed.

It took every ounce of reserve for her to leave the relative safety of the bathroom. Once in the hall, she felt exposed, naked. Her head jerked back and forth. The stairwell door was at the end of the corridor, near the cells.

Sucked a great breath of air and started to move, trying to ignore the stabbing pain. The rooms seemed to creep by. A few doors were open, but they were dark. She knew them well, knew the layout of each one but couldn't see inside. Room Six, the Dungeon. BDSM. Whips and cuffs, stocks, racks.

Several feet away a door opened, and three Visitors poured into the hall. They were distracted, were dragging women out behind them.

Zoey ducked into Room Six, her breath abruptly ripped from her lungs. In the blackness it was impossible to make anything out. Light filtered in through the open door, but her eyes hadn't yet adjusted.

Somebody moaned.

Zoey tried to swallow. No spit. Her throat was parched and raw. Further in, her eyes focused.

Several women were in the room with her. Tamara, who had been here less than a week was strapped to the rack, a large solid wooden platform. Her contorted limbs were stretched to impossible lengths. Kim was hanging upside down against the wall, her ankles in wrist chains. Jessica was hung on rings suspended from the ceiling.

"What the fuck . . . ?" she muttered. She knew the men were demented, but this—

She dry-heaved into her palm. Tears blurred what little vision she had.

"Help . . . " Tamara groaned.

"Zoey?" Jessica cried. "Oh god, Zoey . . . "

"Where are they?" Zoey asked.

Kim was silent, and she wondered with alarm if she was still alive.

"Help . . . " Tamara moaned, her voice a paroxysm of pain.

Zoey returned to the door and listened. The corridor was quiet. Tamara first. She released the crank, loosening the stranglehold on the women's limbs.

Tamara sobbed, thrashed her head on the wooden base.

"Stay still, you have to stop that," she whispered. Tamara's cheek was hot beneath her touch. "Is anything broken? Dislocated?"

"Don't . . . know . . . yet . . . " she moaned, lowering her spastic arms to her side.

Zoey unfastened the clamps next, released Jessica, who slumped to the floor.

Kim was unconscious. Her head dusted the floor, and Zoey lifted it. "Kim? Kim, wake up." She checked for a pulse and found one. Jessica knelt beside them.

"How long has she been hanging here?"

"At least an hour," Jessica said, rubbing the circulation back into her arms. "They raped her, then hung her there."

"Unfasten her ankles. I'll catch her."

Jessica tried to reach up. "My arms, Zoey. No strength in them. I'm sorry."

"Take it easy, Jess, it's okay. Relax for a minute." Zoey lifted Kim's upper body, supported it on her shoulder. She reached up and unfastened the clamps, releasing one foot at a time. Kim's legs came crashing down, but Zoey held her tight, lowered her to the floor.

Tamara crawled over. The four slumped in the corner of the room, useless limbs pressing limbs, temples resting against hair. Kim, still unconscious, was cold and clammy to the touch, her extremities chilled despite the mucky air.

"What the hell do we do now?" Tamara asked through chattery teeth.

"Did they say what they were planning? Did you hear anything at all?" Zoey asked.

"No," Tamara said.

"I heard them talking," Jessica said. "And I saw some of the stuff they brought in."

"Stuff?" The hair on Zoey's arms prickled.

"Torture devices. Like things out of a museum. Or a horror movie. Video equipment too. They were carting it all into Room Twelve."

Room Twelve was sparsely furnished, just a few rings suspended from the ceiling, rubber padding on the floor. The orgy room.

"They were saying how much fun they were going to have. Complaining that James never let them do what they really wanted. The only thing they said to us was 'see you soon, ladies', and then they left. But that was a while ago now."

"They'll be back," Zoey whispered, shivering. "We have to do something."

"Like *what*?" Tamara asked. "They're men, big men, men with guns. What are we supposed to do?"

Zoey shut out the limited light by closing her eyes.

"Where were you hiding, Zoey?" Jessica asked. "They tore this place apart looking for you."

"In the linen closet in the bathroom."

"Linen closet?" Tamara said. "How? Those shelves are tiny."

"It's amazing what you can do when you're desperate. At one point they opened the closet door. I thought I was going to have a stroke."

"Good for you," Tamara said, laughing lightly. "You had them going crazy."

"And they just gave up looking?"

"I guess they had to. They probably figured you escaped somehow."

"I need my shirt," Jessica said. She roamed in the dark room, apparently knowing the layout as well as Zoey did. She retrieved their shirts and handed them out. Zoey slipped one over Kim's head.

"We'll have to be ready for them. When they come back." As the words came out of her mouth, Zoey realized how futile they sounded.

"You have any suggestions?" Tamara said. "They never travel alone, those fuckers. Always in pairs. Or more."

Kim groaned, stirred in Zoey's lap.

"Kim? Can you hear me, Kim?" Zoey took her hand and massaged it between her own.

Kim's head nodded in Zoey's lap. "What . . . ?"

"Long story, Kim. Just rest. Tamara, Jess—let's go." She slid out from beneath Kim, rested her gently on the floor. "Stay here and rest, okay?"

Zoey stood, fighting the return of pain in every tiny bit of movement. The three approached the door, and Zoey closed the gap, leaving it open a couple of inches.

Ear against the tiny opening. "We have to be ready," she whispered. "We'll just have to hope too many don't come back for you. Maybe we can overpower them."

"Oh, *fuck*," Tamara groaned. "That's your plan?"

They waited in silence, sounds of hoarse, rushed breathing, of rattling, abused lungs. Strained for sounds of voices or footsteps.

More time passed, an impossible stretch of endless minutes, leading to the better part of an hour. Zoey's nerves sizzled, felt electrified, adrenaline replacing the blood in her veins.

"Got a plan B?" Tamara muttered, breaking the silence, but Zoey shushed her. Someone was in the hall.

Three men, she could see through the inches-wide gap. Frank she knew. The other two she had seen in the cafeteria but didn't know their names.

"This should be the last of them," Frank said. "I'll get the one in Room Two. Think you can handle these bitches?"

"Jesus, Frank, just go."

"How many are there?" he asked.

"Two. Three. I think we left two." He tittered, briskly massaging his face with his palms. "Too many poppers, Frank! Good coke though. Fucking with my few active brain cells."

Frank shook his head and disappeared down the hall, away from Zoey. The other two men headed toward her.

Two! They'd never overpower these men, especially in their weakened condition. Maybe if they were in better shape, but they were a mess. Beaten, exhausted.

"I gotta take a leak."

"For cryin' out loud, Pete. Now?"

"Yeah, *now*," Pete the one who'd enjoyed too much coke and poppers, whined.

"I'll wait for you. Hurry up."

Pete scratched his head. "Don't wait for me, just go. Unchain them, get them up. I'm not carrying them. Go get started."

"Yeah, but hurry. You're not sticking me with all the shit work again, asshole."

"Yeah, whatever."

Zoey's heart throbbed as he approached the door. The anticipation was like jagged wire digging into her flesh.

He came inside, groped the wall for the light switch. It wasn't beside the door where a switch would traditionally be but was further down the wall.

"Hello, ladies," he said to the torture devices. "Daddy's home." He was fully inside now, his hand sliding up and down the wall. "The fuck are the lights?"

Zoey slammed the door shut, and the elements of darkness and surprise were on her side. She attacked, knocked him off his feet. Sat on his chest and repeatedly bashed him in his face, fought off his fists as they punched her chest. She pinned his arms to his sides with her knees. Someone behind her now, leaning into her—Tamara. She recognized the much larger frame.

"Get the fuck off!" He thrashed beneath her.

"Jessica, get the lights! Tamara, you got him?"

"Yeah, got him!" she panted.

A second later light exploded into life, blinding Zoey.

"Get *off!*"

"Fuck!" Jessica cried. "They'll hear him."

"No, soundproof." Zoey punched him again, glanced back. Tamara was sitting on his legs, and she leaned forward, groped his waist.

The gun.

"Get off me, you fat cunt!"

"Jessica, get something to stuff in his mouth." Well-aimed spittle flew from Zoey's lips, landed on his cheek. "Fuck you."

Jessica returned with the first-aid kit and stuffed gauze in his mouth, wound surgical tape around his head.

"That other asshole will be here any second," Zoey said. "He just went to use the bathroom."

"What should we do with this one?" Tamara said. "Can't shoot him—too much noise."

"Unzip his pants," Zoey said. "Hurry. Pull them down. Underwear too." When Tamara finished, Zoey said, "Now get up, and hold the gun on him. We'll shoot the fucker if we have to. Won't bother me one bit."

Tamara climbed off, and the gagged man started to buck, kicked his legs, tried to throw Zoey off. She leaned back and grabbed his testicles. Immediately his movements stopped. She squeezed, tightened the grip. He grunted, spasmed once.

"Now get up. Nice and easy." She slid off his torso, her hand a deathgrip on his balls, and she led him off the floor. Walked him across the room that way, directed him to the rack.

"Jess, tie him down."

His wrists and ankles were secured, and he screamed into the gag.

Zoey rushed to the front of the room, Tamara directly behind her. "We'll have to do this again in a minute. Kill the lights and—"

But Pete burst into the room.

102

"Kurt! Kurt! Guess what I found! Bloody rags, and a toilet full of-"

For a moment nobody moved. Just stared at one another in shock, until Pete broke the freeze.

"Ah, shit!" he said, reaching for the gun jutting from his waistband.

Zoey attacked, slamming into the wall, pinning him back. He recovered quickly and yanked the gun out of his pants. She grabbed his wrist, and they struggled for control.

Tamara charged his legs, knocking him off balance. The gun flew out of his hand and clattered out of reach on the floor. He lost his footing and landed hard on his ass, grunting.

Tamara pounced, flying through the air like some overgrown trapeze artist and landed solidly on his stomach, every drop of air squeezed out of his lungs, all two hundred fifty plus pounds pinning him down. His hands slammed the floor, punched violently at her as he frantically tried to draw a breath. She pressed harder, not allowing him the luxury of air.

His skin tone changed from magenta to eggplant to grayish blue. Even after it was apparent he was dead, she wouldn't get up.

"Way to go," Zoey said, grinning. "You can get up, Tamara. He's dead."

"I-I can't," she said, voice quivering. Her T-shirt had ridden up, exposing fleshy, cocoa butt cheeks. "I'm sh-shaking too much."

"Okay then, take it easy." She closed the door, looked back. "You gonna fuck him, or what?"

Tamara coughed, slowly rolled off his corpse.

Across the room, Jessica was tightening the tension on the rack restraints. Zoey remembered a story she'd heard as a child, about a demented family that lived in the woods and would capture wayward travelers wandering the dusty back road. The traveler would be tested on the rack. If his limbs were too long, they would chop pieces away until he was a perfect fit. If he was too short, his arms and legs were stretched, tearing from his body, until he became the perfect length for the rack. The rare, lucky man was the one who was already the perfect length, and they would let him go.

Kurt screamed as his wrists were stretched to agonizing lengths. Screams that were muffled by the gag, and rose up from his throat. Movement had become agony, so he stopped thrashing.

"Want me to sit on that asshole, too?" Tamara asked.

"No," Jessica said. "This one's mine." She fondled his swollen testicles, and squashed them, her face reddening with the strain. Tears streamed out of his eyes.

Tamara struggled to her feet, yanked her T-shirt over her ample frame. "'One more turn of the rack, baby'. Isn't that what you said to me before, asshole?" She hovered over him, spit in his face.

He sobbed, turned his head from side to side, eyes pleading.

Jessica cranked the handle, having to use her body to propel it. One more powerful jerk and they heard a pop!, saw his shoulder dislocate.

The ruptured testicle was the least of his problems. Tiny blood vessels exploded on his cheeks, his red face tinged with blue, every muscle in his neck corded.

"Now what?" Tamara asked.

"We've got guns," Zoey said. "Let's use them."

Chapter 13

Forming a plan was next to impossible because they didn't know what they were up against. Didn't know where the other men were, what they were doing.

The four women sat propped beside or against the closed door because it didn't lock, and they didn't need any more surprises.

"Been a long time now," Tamara said. "Someone's bound to come by to see what's going on."

"That's true," Zoey said. She'd started bleeding again and was using Pete's shirt to staunch the flow. "I doubt they'll come one at a time. We're not that lucky. Hey, when you guys were in the cafeteria, how many of them were there?"

"Eight, maybe more." Jessica sighed, massaging her temples. "And they all had guns."

Kim yawned, stretched. "Sorry I missed all the fun tonight. Wish I could have seen you all in action."

"You were really out of it, baby," Tamara said, rubbing Kim's shoulder.

"I thought I was going to die. It was impossible to breathe. These guys aren't fooling around."

"You have a plan, Zoey?" Jessica asked.

"I was thinking about the observation room above Room

Two." Zoey picture the layout, and tried to imagine a way down the endless corridor to reach the stairwell to the observation room. "They seem to be gathered there. But that door's usually locked."

"They unlocked everything," Tamara said. "Most of the doors are open. They must know what's up there. They're probably using it. They had video equipment, and that's a perfect spot to shoot from."

"That's our best chance," Zoey said.

"If you get caught up there, you're trapped. No way out, probably." Kim's voice was weak.

"You can say that about any area down here. No place is safe. Sitting in here ain't safe." Tamara stood, went to check on Kurt, tied to the rack. He'd stopped struggling a while ago and emitted a constant low-grade whine.

"Here's my idea," Zoey said. "Kim stays and rests. She's no use to us right now."

Kim opened her mouth but Zoey shook her head. "They nearly killed you, Kim, and you're too out of it to go hunting. I'll take a gun and see if I can get upstairs. Tamara, Jessica, you stay here and try to handle whatever comes through that door."

"Uh uh, I'll go with you," Tamara said. "You might need help."

"Kim needs help right now. And Jessica won't be ale to handle the men by herself. We really can't use the guns, unless we have no alternative. Gunshots would bring them running, and then we're dead for sure."

Tamara sat beside them, crossed her thick legs at the ankles and pulled her T-shirt over her knees.

Jessica looked from Kurt to Pete, then back to the women. "If those guys see this, we're all dead."

No one responded to that. Zoey imagined they were all experiencing the same fear and dread that had consumed her.

"Let's go," Zoey said, getting up. "Let's do this."

Kim leaned against the wall, doubled over. Tamara led her to the corner of the room and made her lie down.

"Be on alert," Zoey said. The gun felt massive, and it scared her. She'd never held one before. Living in New York City, she'd never had the need for one. Pistol permits were nearly impossible to get unless you had a dangerous, high profile job, one where you needed security. As a computer technician, there wasn't much reason for her to own a gun.

"Safety off," Jessica said, pointing at the pistol. "Otherwise you won't get far."

"Safety?" Zoey studied the firearm, had no clue where the safety was.

Jessica pointed it out. "It's a Beretta. Slide that back. Cock the hammer, aim and shoot. Simple."

Zoey smiled, rolled her eyes. "Yes, simple. Sure. Piece of cake." She tossed Pete's bloody shirt on his corpse. She rested against the door for a moment, building courage to turn the knob, to take that first step outside the security blanket of the room.

She nodded once, peered into the hall. Empty.

The stairwell leading to the observation area was at the far end of the hall, above Room Two, about thirty feet away.

Took that first step out, her toes touching the cold tiles. Slowly at first, she walked past open doors that revealed nothing but dark, gaping maws. Moved faster, feet slapping, sounding like thunderclaps in the stillness of the corridor.

She was nearly there when a door she had just passed suddenly opened.

Bile filled her throat as she panicked. No place to hide, not even a tiny alcove to stuff herself into. A searing pain shot through her temples, and she leaned into the wall as if hoping to be obscured by it.

Two men stepped into the hall, facing away from her. She recognized one as Jeff, the freak from the nursery who liked to watch. The one who had pissed on her. They started walking down the hall, in the direction she had just come from. She held her breath, her body trembling, and she desperately wanted to scream.

"Close the goddamned door," Jeff said. "You raised in a barn or something?"

"Fuck it, let *them* close it. I'm sick of this shit Zack's got us doing. I didn't agree to this when I paid my goddamned fortune."

The sound of Jeff's laughter followed them down the hall.

Her legs didn't want to work. She forced herself to turn, to make it the last few feet to the stairwell.

The door was open. Once inside, she listened for movement. No voices, but heard the humming of equipment, and a light slapping sound.

The old wooden staircase was solidly built, and she hoped it wouldn't creak. One step, stop, listen. Then another. She didn't know the layout of the room above. If someone was there, would she see his face, or his back?

The gun nearly slipped from her slick fingers. Sweat trickled down her face. Three more steps to the top. Two. The next step would bring her near the landing, would expose her head.

She couldn't do this. Every nerve in her body was charged, every muscle over-wound. Every step a discovery in self reliance.

Maybe it wasn't too late to turn back. Maybe they'd forgive her, go easy on her.

Maybe they'd torture and kill her.

One more step. Tiny step.

She forced the step, and peered over the edge. Discovered the source of the slapping noise.

He was sitting in a swivel chair, deeply engrossed in whatever was happening below. His engorged cock was in his hand, and he was beating off. His body was at an angle, not quite facing away.

She waited. He threw back his head and groaned, pounded harder. Cum spurted onto his hand, and he was lost in the throes of orgasm.

Zoey sprang up behind him. Seized his testicles, clamped down.

His eyes popped open, then his mouth, a look of utter shock on his face. "What the fuck?" He tried to move away but she squeezed tighter, and he doubled over. She pressed the gun against the back of his head.

"Don't move, or I'll rip them right off and shove them down your throat."

Now what? She hadn't thought this would work and didn't have part two planned.

"... the fuck?" he muttered.

"Shut your mouth," she hissed, pressing the gun harder, at the same time applying more pressure to his balls.

His gun rested on the console a few feet away.

"I'm going to start moving you to the floor. I suggest you follow, unless you want two foot testicles. Nice and slow now." Pulled him in the direction she wanted and he followed, his hands splayed out in front of his body.

She raised her arm and cocked it back, and with a powerful swing smashed him in the back of his head with the gun.

He collapsed the rest of the way, landing hard. Blood seeped from the head wound.

She pulled her hand out from beneath his body, hoping he was unconscious, no way to know for certain. Using extension cords she yanked from outlets, carefully watching him every few seconds, she tightly bound his hands and feet. Her gun was on the floor beside her, inches away, but he didn't move.

Using a third cord, she hog-tied his hands and feet together behind his back. Grabbed the towel draped on the back of the chair and stuffed part of it in his mouth, wrapped the rest around his head and tied it at the back of his neck.

She raced downstairs and closed and locked the door. Rushed back up. Her prisoner hadn't moved.

Video cameras mounted on tripods or secured to posts were recording the room below. She reached to shut them off but changed her mind. If she somehow survived this, the tapes would be evidence.

Zoey looked at the room below the observation area. Horrified, her mouth fell open.

Chapter 14

Everyone was there, other than the three she left behind in Room Six. The women, guards, Visitors, even James. The torture devices Jessica had described were in the room as well, and they were in use.

Dizzying waves overpowered her, and she gripped the console. Couldn't watch this, had never seen anything like it. On the panel she noticed the volume button and turned it on.

Screams poured out of the speaker, voices yelling and laughing, the sounds of whips and belts destroying flesh. The whirring of drills followed by shrieks.

"No . . . " she sobbed, sucking air, shaking her head. Brushed away tears and looked again at the carnage.

Women chained, hanging from walls and ceiling, some upside down. Being beaten and raped. A shrill scream drowned out the voices for a moment. Marie, tied to a beam, her nipples being burned by a cigarette lighter. Cathy, tied spread-eagle to rings jutting from the floor, was approached by a man handling a grotesquely oversized dildo.

Some had been so severely beaten, their faces swollen and hidden by gore, that Zoey didn't recognize them.

In a section of the room, Megan was tied to rings jutting from the floor. Her joints were being pulverized by a man wielding a hammer, and he methodically smashed bone after bone, bits of white, sharp cartilage poking through purple flesh. Her screams of torment were drowned by the noise in the room, by the pounding of the hammer.

They unchained her from the floor and threaded her mashed limbs through the spokes of an oversized wagon wheel, strapping her in place, securing her. Moments later they began to beat her with a bullwhip.

Zack stood at the front of the room, easily ignoring the crying and begging women. "Dinner's ready," he said. "Why don't you guys—"

The door to the torture chamber was slammed open, and Tamara and Jessica came stumbling inside.

"Oh, no . . . " Zoey said, getting up. "Oh, god, no . . . "

Jeff followed them in.

"What's wrong?" Zack said.

Jeff gestured wildly. "Pete's dead. Kurt's nearly dead. You should see what the fuck they did to them. That black bitch tried to sit on me but I moved away too fast."

"What *happened*?" Zack said, grabbing Jeff's shoulders.

"They were loose in there, attacking everyone who went in."

"*What*?" Zack looked at Tamara and Jessica. Other than the moans from those unable to help themselves, all other noise had ceased.

Zack grabbed Jessica's hair and yanked back her head. "How did you get loose?"

Wide-eyed, Jessica stammered, threw her hands up to lessen his painful grip. He threw her to the floor.

He approached Tamara. "Tell me."

She stood defiantly, didn't seem like she was going to tell him anything until he punched her in the face. Arms pinwheeling, she went flying and landed on her back. He kicked her in her side. "Answer me, you cunt."

"My hand got loose from the binding," she cried, cowering.

"What binding?"

"I was on the rack," she sobbed. "It loosened, and I slipped my hand out." She sat up slowly, rubbed her cheek.

The men gathered around Zack. Face scarlet, as if with fever, he glowered at Tamara and Jessica. "What did they do to them, Jeff?"

"Pete's dead. Looks like he was crushed. Kurt's on the rack. Nearly torn apart."

"Dead?"

"No, not yet. But he's a mess. Balls are crushed, joints nearly ripped out of his sockets."

"Leave him for now. We'll get a doctor down here."

"I think he needs a hospital," Jeff said, scratching his ear.

"No hospitals. I'll get him a doctor. But we've got some business to take care of first." He glanced around the room, as if deciding on a plan of action.

"James gets a reprieve. Tamara here gets to take his place. And this one—Jessica—she gets the splitter."

They lifted Jessica, screaming, flipped her upside down, and chained her ankles into two widely-spaced cuffs hanging from the ceiling, her head brushing the floor. A large hand-held saw was brought over.

Zack genuflected beside her head. "This is an old-fashioned execution method. Quite ingenious in its simplicity. The idea is that in your position, the blood drains from the body and rushes to the head. When we start to saw between your legs, there will be very little blood loss, so your death will be agonizing and incredibly slow. We'll slice right here." His fingers brushed her mound for emphasis. "Right in your slit. Slowly make our way down, very . . . very . . . slowly. It'll be a while before we reach any arteries or major organs. This will take an eternity, Jessica."

Jessica sobbed, twisting in the cuffs, her hands spread on the floor to relieve the pressure.

Zack took away the shirt that had pooled around her head. "I wouldn't want you to miss seeing anything."

"And you," he said, approaching Tamara, "what did you think you were going to do? Save everyone? Is that what you are, a savior?" He stroked her chin, and she yanked her head back. "Well, *savior*, you'll meet the same fate as our last Savior."

Large wooden beams were dragged to the center of the room. Behind that, another man carried a large rubber mallet and a box of carpenter nails.

Tamara moaned, sank to her knees. Zack laughed. "Here's your chance for martyrdom, Savior."

"What about him?" Jeff pointed toward James. "I thought he was going to be crucified."

Zack pulled out a cigarette and lit it. Shrugged. "Plan B, then. We'll think of something. I didn't bring enough wood to do two, and she deserves it more than he does."

Zack then addressed the rest of the men. "Go back to what you were doing. No need to stop enjoying yourselves. I'll let you know when I'm ready."

One by one they returned to the women.

Zoey studied the room. In the corner sat the former guards, hands and feet bound. They weren't going to be any help. Even if they weren't bound, she doubted they'd be useful.

Beside Jessica now, he licked two fingers and thrust, fucked her with them, jamming them deep. Then he added another finger, then a fourth, twisting and turning his hand until it disappeared. He grinned, seeming to enjoy her screams, her spastic jerks. Brutally raped her with his fist, left it in there as he spoke to Jeff.

"Still too much blood. She'll die too quickly if we cut now." Jeff nodded.

"Hey, go fuck something, would you?"

Jeff snorted, grinned, walked toward the massacre.

Jessica's blood dripped off Zack's hand when he pulled it out. A plan, she needed a plan, but Zoey's mind wasn't cooperating. If she went in shooting, there was no telling who she might kill. The idea to wait until the men went to bed crossed her mind, but Tamara and Jessica would probably be dead by then. And there was no telling when these men would need to get some sleep. It seemed as if they were wired.

Crying wasn't much help, but she couldn't control it. This was too much, it wasn't fair! How was she supposed to help those women?

Zack's voice pulled her out of her crying jag. He was testing Jessica's blood flow again with his fist, and said to the man with the mallet, "This is taking too goddamned long, Doug. How long does it take blood to drain to the head?"

Doug hoisted the mallet over his shoulder like a lumberjack. "I don't know, Zack. What about that dinner you mentioned? We can eat, do her when we get back."

Zack clapped him on the back. "Guys, listen up."

Some of the men looked, a couple were too busy. Zack waited for them to finish. A minute later he had everyone's attention.

"Let's grab something to eat. When we come back, we'll have our crucifixion and our sawing ceremony. I need two of you to stay here and stand guard." He lit another unfiltered cigarette.

"Why?" Frank, the one who had beaten Zoey with the belt in the nursery, asked Zack. He pointed at Tamara. "You worried about that one? Put a fucking bullet in her brain, man. Or at least chain her up somewhere."

"She's escaped once already. I'm not taking any chances."

"Then why don't we do the crucifixion first?" Serge asked, patting his fat stomach. "It sure would give me an appetite."

Zack didn't answer for a moment. Took a drag of his cigarette, shrugged. "Why not? It'll get her out of the way. Line up the wood."

Men dragged the planks to the center of the room, and from the floor, Tamara began to scream.

"Shut up!" Zack yelled, kicked her in the stomach with his

boot. Tamara doubled over and fell on her side.

Serge yanked her shirt off. Rolled her onto her back, her enormous breasts sliding to the outsides of her chest. He yanked his cock a few times, spread her legs. Raped her to the sounds of pounding nails, fucked with the rhythm of hammer strikes.

She didn't move. Didn't scream or try to push him off, as if she had given up.

Serge pulled out, looked up at the circle of men surrounding them, and climbed off, using her stomach for support.

They grabbed her arms and feet and dragged her to the boards, now nailed together in the shape of a cross, centered her on it.

Arms stretched across the wood, palms up. Small pieces of plywood were laid on her hands.

"Please, no . . . " she groaned.

"Hold her. Doug? Let's go." Zack squashed his cigarette beneath his boot.

Gripped the mallet like he was choking up on a bat, then raised it overhead. A carpenter nail was held in place, and Doug swung, pounding the nail through her flesh, into the wood. Tamara screeched, her body bucking. Several men held her in place, sat on her flailing body. Another swing of the mallet, and the nail was buried. Sprays of blood covered Doug, the floor, the man holding the nail.

He moved to her other hand, pounded in the nail.

Ashen complexion, a luster of sweat covering her body. No more screams; the shock had taken over.

Several other women were crying and screaming, begging them to stop.

Tamara's legs were pushed together, ankles placed one on top of the other. Doug pulled a spike out of his pocket, handed it over. A small piece of wood was laid on top of her feet, and the spike was pounded in. They reinforced her wrists and ankles with rope, securing her firmly to the cross.

"Gonna need help with this," Frank said. "We have to lift her."

The men groaned.

"Couldn't you find someone smaller to crucify?" Serge bitched.

"Oh, but she was okay to fuck, right, Serge?" Zack said.

Serge turned away.

Four men leaned over, grabbed the cross by the arms. One footed the base while the others lifted, pushing it upright. They dragged it to a nearby support beam and propped it.

"*Now* we can eat," Zack said. "I still want one guard in here. Volunteers?"

"I'll stay," Serge said. "Fuck, Zack, it's better than eating whatever you've cooked."

Zack laughed. "Good man. Someone want to go get Ralph?"

Zoey's heart stopped when Zack looked up at her. "Hey, Ralph?" Filled with terror, wondered if he could see her through the glass.

"Ralph? Can you hear me up there?"

She didn't know what to do.

"Ralph?"

She banged on the glass. Zack nodded.

"We're going to grab dinner. Come on down."

"He can eat with me," Serge said. "Keep me company."

Zack looked up again. "You mind waiting? Bang on the glass if you'll wait to eat with Serge."

Zoey banged on the glass.

"Good. Hey, Serge, think you can find something to keep yourself busy?"

Serge smiled, shrugged. "I'll think of something."

Zack pointed at Jessica. "Do me a favor and check her once in a while. See how the blood flow is coming along. I want to start sawing when we get back."

The women had been deserted in awkward, painful

positions, limbs stretched and contorted, genitalia burned or whipped beyond recognition. Head slumped forward, blood and pus oozing from grisly wounds, Tamara moaned nonstop.

Zoey hefted the pistol, and reached across the panel to grab her prisoner's gun.

Chapter 15

Huddled at the head of the stairs, gun aimed at dead air, Zoey waited. Ralph's gun was on the floor beside her, not even a waistband to tuck it in, only the T-shirt on her back. Ralph's pants might have fit, but she wasn't about to untie him to remove his clothes.

The door downstairs was open a bit, which she'd done a minute earlier, hoping to avoid suspicion. Bursts of laughter and conversation flew up from the corridor. Zoey swallowed, and raised the gun in shivering hands. Death would be certain if they were to come up now, but she planned to take as many with her as she could.

But the voices faded, trailed until they became nothing. She cried out in relief, wiped the back of her hand across her forehead.

Ralph moved, grunted into his gag. Looked into her blue eyes, pleaded with his own. Babbling into the gag as she approached him, bobbing his head, groaning. The words were unintelligible but she knew what he wanted.

"Not a chance in Hell, buddy," she whispered as she cracked the butt of the pistol on his head. Out cold again, blood gushing from his newest wound.

Through the two-way glass, she watched Serge stroking himself, standing in the center of the room. Looking from woman to woman as if sampling a buffet, deciding what he wanted to try first.

In the corner, a severely beaten James was either sleeping or dead. The guards beside him were tightly bound, and gagged, but they didn't look badly hurt. No missing limbs, no major blood loss.

Not much time to act. With Serge distracted, she might have a chance.

Guns in both hands, Zoey crept down the steps and reached the door. Chewed her lip, slowly peered outside the room. The door opened out, into the corridor, and she peeked behind it to make sure no one was there.

Beside her, the door to Room Two. Turned the knob, stole inside as quietly as possible, hoping Serge was still distracted. His attention was focused on Marie, chained to the back wall.

The door snicked shut, and she searched for a weapon to use other than the guns. Something quiet, something that wouldn't make an explosive noise.

Strewn about the room, assortments of belts, whips, bats, clubs, paddles, wooden sticks like mop handles. In order to use the quieter weapon, she would have to get rid of one of the guns. Both, if she wanted to wield it effectively.

She wrinkled her nose. The air was steamy with the stench of blood and shit and vomit. She had gotten used to her own pissy smell.

No option left but to drop the guns, and laid them on the floor, grabbed a bat.

The glassy-eyed women who had noticed her now had hope in their eyes, mouths ringed in expressions of pain and wonder. Zoey held her finger up to her lips.

Serge was raping Marie now, her screams muffled by his large hand, his pig grunts and laughter chilling Zoey's bones.

She charged across the floor, bat raised high overhead, and smashed him across his back. He slumped forward, crushing Marie to the wall.

The bat nearly slipped from her slick fingers as she bashed him again and again, the last time splitting his skull. Struck him several more times. Crimson spray covered her face, her shirt, Marie, the wall. For a moment he seemed suspended in mid-air, and then slowly slid down the length of Marie's body, crashed to the floor, his dead face a rictus of shock.

Marie started to laugh and cry, her chest rapidly rising and falling, tongue jutting between clenched teeth. Zoey unclamped her wrists and released her from the wall.

"Hurry!" Zoey's voice was a loud, strained whisper. "Get everyone untied. We don't have much time." She retrieved one of the guns.

She and Marie rushed around the room, releasing the women. Moans of relief were deafening, and Zoey kept trying to get them to quiet down. With Marie's help, she lifted Jessica and released her ankles, gently lowering the unconscious woman to the floor.

"Jesus," Marie muttered. "What smells so bad?"

"That would be me," Zoey said. She glanced at the guards, tied up a few feet away. "What do you think? How about them?"

"I think they'd help." Their heads bobbed in frantic agreement.

Zoey frowned, scratched her head. "I think we need all the help we can get. We have to get Tamara down from that goddamned cross. What about James?"

Marie started to untie the guards. "They can help us with Tamara. James is a mess. Probably won't matter either way. He won't be much use."

James's eyes were swollen shut, and he was slumped on his side. His hands were blue from the lack of circulation from excessively tight bonds. Zoey untied him, checked his pulse. Still alive.

Claudia, who had been rescued from a bondage mask, arms chained behind her, nipple clamps holding her still, had retrieved a gun and now controlled it as if she'd held one before. Powerfully muscled legs shoulder-width apart. Face streaked with gore, fresh burns on her stomach, blood oozing from her damaged nipples, the five-foot-ten woman looked ready for battle. Or as if she had already survived one.

"What's the plan?" Claudia asked, moving beside Zoey, never taking her eyes off the door.

"No plan. Just winging it." Zoey looked up from her spot kneeling beside James. "Look like you've done this before. Know how to handle that thing?"

"Hell yeah! New York State Trooper."

Zoey grinned. "Good!"

T-shirts were being distributed, wounded prisoners being triaged, tended to as best as possible using the small first-aid kit.

Claudia laid her gun on the floor to pull the shirt on over her head.

The door suddenly opened and a man wandered in, distracted, sucking his teeth. "Hey Serge? Zack wants to know if—Holy shit!"

Before anyone could react, he pulled the gun out of his waistband. "Nobody fucking move! Freeze!" He looked at Zoey, at the gun in her hand. "Put it on the floor." He stepped into the room. His hands were shaking, but he looked excited.

"You must be that cunt Zoey." He grinned. "We're going to enjoy peeling the skin off your body, you stupid bitch."

She never had a chance to raise her gun. Slowly stood, her heart hammering, body slick with sweat. "Listen, this is all my fault, not theirs."

"Shut the fuck up. Give me that goddamned gun. Slide it over here. And where's Serge?"

Oh god . . . Words just wouldn't come, no matter how much she tried to force them. Her tongue was a slab of dead meat on the bottom of her mouth. She could only hope her death would be painless but began to see less and less of a chance of that happening. For a moment she tried to imagine someone peeling the skin off her body, and she shuddered, her stomach churning acid.

"Answer me!"

"We locked him in the bathroom," Zoey stammered.

"Where's the key?"

"In the lock."

"Bullshit. You're a fucking liar." Sweat glimmered on his balding head. It seemed he didn't know what he wanted to do. Licked his lips, head jerking, scanning the room. At least thirty people—women, former guards, all prisoners now—glowered back. But he had the guns.

"Everyone sit down! Not you," he told Zoey.

She stood defiantly, despite her watery legs and a stomach trying to empty itself of everything she had ever eaten.

"Wait! You—kick that gun over here."

Claudia did as he instructed and the gun spun near his feet.

"This is priceless," he said, running his hand over his slick scalp. "Do you have any idea what we're going to do to you?"

"Some idea. You goddamned coward. All of you are shit!"

The stunned look on his face was priceless, would be forever etched in Zoey's memory. "Keep talking, bitch. You're making it worse." He picked up the gun Claudia had kicked over, restored the safety and tucked the spare weapons into his belt.

"You—" He pointed at Claudia." You look good and strong. Come here." Claudia stuck her tongue in her cheek and approached him.

"Pick that up." The mallet. She did as he said.

"You—Zoey. Lay down. Right here."

This didn't look good. No, this was a fucking mess. She lifted her hands, protesting. He raised the gun and pointed it at her head. The room was spinning . . . jagged shards of light stabbed her eyes. Her legs turned to mush. Slowly, she lowered herself to the floor, head pounding, dry-heaving, and lay down.

Pointed the gun at Claudia's head. "Break her leg. Right below the knee."

The mallet slipped, almost fell from Claudia's hands.

"Do it! If you disobey me, you won't be able to imagine what I'll do to you."

Her complexion was ashy. "I can't . . . "

Pulled the hammer back on the gun, pointed it at her. "Oh, you can't?"

Claudia raised the mallet.

He stepped back, gun aimed at her head. Claudia sobbed. "I'm so sorry, Zoey!" Raised the mallet two-fisted over her head.

Zoey squeezed her eyes shut, waited for the unimaginable pain. *Crack!* Opened them again when she felt nothing.

Her tormentor, on his knees, blood tricking down his scalp. Behind him stood Kim, sporting a metal pipe in both hands, chest heaving, spattered blood freckling her face.

"Oh, Jesus," Zoey muttered, shaking so badly she couldn't move.

Claudia grabbed the three guns from his belt, and from where he had dropped one. Kim knelt beside Zoey, helped her sit up. She threw her arms around Kim's neck and sobbed.

Claudia shut the door. The room exploded in cheers. "Where's that fat fuck's gun?" she said, heading toward Serge's body.

"I forgot about you, Kim." Behind her, people were carefully lowering a crucified Tamara to the floor.

"Where were you? Why didn't they find you?" Zoey asked.

"I hid beneath the rack, right below that asshole. The guys came in and untied him, but he was a babbling mess. He barely knew where he was, never mind me. And those guys are so strung out on god-knows-what they didn't remember who they'd left behind."

"Where did you find the pipe?" Zoey asked, testing its weight in her hands, avoiding the smear of blood decorated with flecks of scalp.

"Upstairs. I went looking for you and found that guy instead. Your handiwork I presume? I saw what was happening down here and looked for a weapon."

Claudia returned. "We've got five guns. Not too bad. And we're slowly eliminating those scumbags. How many are left?"

"Four or five I think," Zoey said. "And five down so far."

"Five?"

"These two, two in the room where they had Tamara, Jess and Kim, and one upstairs in observation. I took care of that one. I think nine came in originally, right?"

Claudia nodded. "I think it was nine, maybe ten."

"Any chance they have guards posted upstairs?" Zoey asked.

"Not likely," Claudia said. "There wouldn't be a need for guards, right? These cocky bastards probably figured they were just dealing with a group of women and a handful of unarmed guards. Nothing they couldn't handle."

She turned to the former guards, who were huddled in a corner, wisely staying out of Zoey's way. "How do we get out of this place?"

Chapter 16

Larry—whose name they learned after checking his wallet—was dragged to the rack and strapped down. After half a dozen cranks he began to scream, so someone stuffed a shirt in his mouth to gag him.

"They're taking too long to eat," Claudia said. She crossed her arms and rubbed her shoulders, her teeth chattering. "They should have been back by now."

"We need to send someone to check," Zoey said.

Kim shook her head. "Too dangerous. If someone goes out there, she could get caught."

"Ideas then?" Zoey glanced around the room. Even the badly injured seemed excited, alive. Tamara had been removed from the cross, her horrible wounds bandaged as best as possible by Marie, a doctor before she was kidnapped. The first-aid kit was now empty. Everywhere around the room women sported bandages, antiseptic, and burn cream.

"I can listen at the door. See if anyone's coming. We should have someone there anyway," Kim said.

Zoey nodded.

"Let's talk to the guards," Claudia said, pushing her hair behind her ears.

The guards were the lesser of two evils and were still regarded with disdain. Untying them hadn't seemed like a good idea, so they bound their hands again.

"Quiet everyone," Zoey said. Conversations stopped. "Kim's going to guard the door, to see if they're coming back. That means the door will be open, so everyone has to keep real quiet."

The guards cowered when Zoey and Claudia approached them. James was conscious now, blinking dried blood of his lashes, his eyes so swollen they barely opened.

"How do we get out of here?" Claudia asked. "Where's the exit?"

Heads bowed, turned away. One cleared his throat. Nobody was volunteering information.

"Goddammit," Claudia snapped. "Don't you get it? This is over. We're not your prisoners anymore. Now tell us how to get out if this fucking hellhole."

Robin, former-prisoner-turned-guard, the one who had raped Zoey with a nightstick, scowled, snapped her hair out of her eyes. "It doesn't work that way."

"What way?" Zoey asked, aching to kick her, punch her, anything. "What are you talking about?"

"You'll never get past Zack," Robin said. "He's a goddamned drug lord, for Christ's sake. And if by some miracle you do, we'll all be in trouble. You'll go to the cops."

"I got news for you, sweetheart," Claudia said, prodding her with her bare foot. "I *am* the cops. You kidnapped, raped, and tortured a cop. Have any idea what they'll do to you in prison? If you make it to prison."

Zoey elbowed her. "You're not helping, here . . . " But she smiled, knowing that Robin probably wouldn't have said anything helpful anyway. "Look, guys, there's only one way we'll survive this, and that's through the exit. In case you haven't noticed, you're mixed up in all of this, too. You think they'll just let you walk out of here?"

"Sure," Tony said. Dried blood was smeared across his lip.

"They won't do anything to us. They know we can't turn them in. What would we say to the cops? That the men we brought in to rape the women we'd already kidnapped turned on us? That'd go over well."

"Are you kidding?" Zoey said. "Look at yourselves. You really think you would have survived this? They can't take any chance of one of you squealing. Look what they did to James."

James laughed, his face a spasm of pain for his efforts. "They won't tell you anything," he said through swollen, split lips, cracked and bloodied teeth. "Too well paid."

"I'll tell you," Kevin said. Kevin—the only one to show any compassion, the one who had tried to stop Serge and his fellow pigs in the nursery.

"Shut the fuck up," James hissed.

"Fuck you," Kevin said. "Zoey, I'm so sorry about all of this. Believe me when I tell you I had no choice in doing what I did. It's over, James. This has gone on too far."

"You know what'll happen to your kids, Kevin. You want one of your little girls being fucked and tortured down here? They'll be right beside their daddy, their little pussies stretched by giant cocks . . . "

"Fuck you!" he spat. "I'll fucking kill you!"

Zoey gently covered Kevin's mouth with her hand. Said to James, "Tell us how to get out of here, or I swear to god I'll—"

"They're coming!" Kim cried, gently closing the door.

Claudia handed Zoey a gun. Handed one to Kim and Jessica, who had both handled firearms before. They hid behind columns, ducked low.

"Everyone down!" Zoey said, aiming her gun at the door.

An eternity passed before the door finally opened, and two men wandered in before realizing anything was wrong. Claudia took a shot and the bullet removed the top part of Jeff's scalp, jets of blood shooting like a fountain.

Zoey fired, and the bullet chipped away the doorframe over

their heads. The other man reached for his gun, but Kim and Jessica were quicker. One shot him in the thigh, the other in the stomach, and he went down. From behind him, shots were fired into the room.

"Watch out!" Claudia cried, falling to one knee, aiming her gun at the men in the hall.

A bullet whizzed past Zoey's ear. Kim was struck in the shoulder, and the impact knocked her off her feet.

"Kim!" Zoey crawled toward her.

The firing stopped, the men in the hall no longer targets.

Marie ran over and applied pressure to Kim's wound. Others came to help and pulled Kim to a safer part of the room.

The wounded man writhed on the floor like an enormous slug, clutched his injured body parts. Claudia carefully approached, wary of possible gunfire from the hall. She kicked the guns across the floor, toward Zoey.

A cell phone protruded from Jeff's back pocket, and Claudia pulled the door shut before snatching the phone.

Zoey glanced up. The Observation room! "Everyone move to the front of the room. Quickly! Get away from the glass." Frenzied movements from everywhere, the wounded being dragged or carried to the front of the room.

A voice boomed into the room over the loudspeaker. "Very smart."

Zack.

"Wise decision, Zoey. It is *Zoey*, isn't it?"

"Yes, you piece of shit. I'm Zoey."

"How do you propose to get out alive, Zoey?"

"How do *you*?"

The loudspeaker sizzled, but there was no response from Zack.

"He can still hear us," she whispered to Claudia. "I could hear everything when I was up there."

Claudia nodded. Clicked on the cell phone, punched in 9-1-1. Shrugged—nothing.

"No signal this far below ground, Zoey," James muttered. He shifted, propped against the wall. "We're a couple hundred feet below ground. I had this place built years ago. We're in the middle of nowhere, deep in the mountains. Miles from civilization. Even if you manage to somehow escape, you'll never survive the elements." He laughed, then groaned, took a deep breath.

"Shut up already," Zoey muttered.

"I'll show you the way out," James said.

Jerked her head back in his direction, eyed him suspiciously. "You will? Why?"

"Because you need my help. Because you'll never make it out without me. And because I can use this as a bargaining tool."

"Bargain? You're insane."

He licked his swollen lips. "You know I'm insane. But what's this worth to you? Is my immunity worth the price of your freedom?"

"No, James. No way. You're going down."

"Suit yourself, Zoey. But trust me, you won't escape. If you get past Zack, and even if you find the exit, you won't get past it. It's barricaded with a heavy oak door, with a combination keypad. Even my guards don't know the combo."

"You're lying," Zoey whispered.

"Am I?" Grimaced, clutched his stomach. "Why wouldn't I have installed an additional safety measure? You'll never get through it. Better hope I don't die, Zoey, or you're all fucked."

His guards glanced at him.

"Oh, fuck this," Kevin said. "I know the combination."

"Do you?" James sneered. "Because I change it once a week. I changed it yesterday, in fact."

Zoey looked at Claudia. "Know any way to get this information?"

"Because I'm a cop? We don't beat confessions out of people. Anymore." She smiled. "Besides, I doubt it would have much of an impact on him at this point."

"Zack knows the combination," James said coolly. "Why don't you go ask him?"

"Somebody shut him up," Zoey said.

"Know where we are, Zoey?" James asked. "Adirondack Mountains. You have any idea how big the Adirondacks are? How cold it gets at night, even in summer? And here we are, in the dead of winter . . . "

Zoey looked away. Stared at her gun, considered bashing him in the head with it.

"You need my help. That's the bottom line."

She wondered why Zack hadn't made a move. He was outnumbered at this point, but everyone in the room was a target.

She took Claudia aside and whispered in her ear. "The cell phone may work once we get to the surface. Maybe we'll find the way out, and there's bound to be cars. They had to have gotten in and out of here somehow."

"What about Zack and his guys? How can we get past them?" Claudia asked.

"You really think they're still out there? We outnumber them ten to one. We have more guns. There are three of them left. They haven't made a move, and I'd bet they didn't have a plan in mind in case something like this should happen."

Claudia nodded, scratched her nose. "What do you want to do?"

"We have to check it out. Two of us with guns need to do a search."

"I'll go with you."

Zoey nodded. She and Claudia approached the other women and quietly shared their plan. Out of view of the glass, she hoped Zack, if he was still upstairs, hadn't heard anything.

"Get him up," Claudia said, and the gut-shot man was pulled to his feet. She cracked the door, using him as a shield. Tossed him into the hallway as a diversion and he crashed into the opposite wall head first.

"Let's go," she said, gun poised, and stepped into the corridor. Checked left, right. No sign of movement as Zoey followed her out.

They walked back to back. No sign of life other then the wounded man moaning, writhing against the wall.

They reached the door to the Observation room. "I need to check it out."

Zoey nodded, shuddered, goosebumps creeping up her arms.

"Guard the door. I'm going up." Claudia drew a deep breath, scoped out the flight of stairs, and ducked into the bottom landing.

Head spinning, Zoey waited out the eternal minutes. The adrenaline still pumped through her veins like a drug, but she felt strangely calm. Empowered. Ready to face her own death, if need be. There was no going back now.

Claudia reappeared. "It's secure," she whispered. "One guy up there. Bound, gagged, throat slashed. Your handiwork I presume."

Zoey shook her head in surprise. "I didn't kill him."

"They apparently don't want witnesses. They'd rather kill their own guy."

Zoey slumped against the wall. "What if they're hiding in one of the rooms? How are we supposed to check over a dozen dark rooms?"

"I'll be right back." Claudia disappeared up the stairs again. Less than a minute later she was back. "Master light switches. Power generator."

"How'd you know?"

"I've been in this place a long time. Heard them talking, and I've noticed the generators and emergency lights. Makes sense, this far underground. Can't rely on electricity."

"At least the rooms are lit now. Let's get started."

With agonizing slowness they checked each room, Zoey standing guard at the door while Claudia searched. Every room they inspected, including the bathrooms was empty, except Room Six, where they had left Pete dead and Kurt tied down to the rack. Now Kurt was dead as well, but with the amount of blood on his body, Zoey didn't know if she was responsible for his death or if he had been executed.

Room Four. *Punishment*. The room she had luckily never had to face, the one where hysterical women were threatened with, dragged into.

The door was closed, unlike the others. She licked her lips and reached out with tentative fingers . . . unable to imagine the horror of what James would consider punishment . . . what other deviation could he have concocted that would be worse than what they had already survived?

Turned the knob . . . the door creaked open.

Inside, leaning against one corner, a mop and broom. Small sink on the opposite side of the tiny room.

Zoey expelled a sigh of disbelief.

"A goddamned closet," Claudia muttered.

James had terrified them with a utility closet.

They reached the cafeteria. Claudia checked it, as well as the kitchen and pantry. Came out a few minutes later. "Empty."

"I hope this means they're gone. Where the hell is the exit? Have you ever seen a way out? Or how they come in?"

Claudia shook her head. "We were released from the cells after everyone was already here. There's that freak Sullivan's office. Maybe it's there. We need to check the cells too, even though that would be a stupid place for them to hide."

One door down the short hall, near the cafeteria, led to the cells. The door beside it led to Sullivan's office. She hadn't seen him since the coup, but he only showed up a couple times a week anyway.

Zoey opened the cell door, Claudia flanking her, gun held two-fisted and chin high. No movement inside. Claudia entered, searched. It would have been easy to spot anyone hiding, even beneath the cots.

The sight of the cells made Zoey's knees weak. For some reason, seeing them disturbed her more than seeing the torture rooms. Especially strong, now that she had a renewed taste of freedom, the cells represented everything about this underground torture chamber, the confinement, the despair, the utter hopelessness.

They reached the one door they had not yet checked.

"Ready?" Claudia whispered.

No, she wasn't ready. Her palms were slick, fingers sticky, the gun trying to slip from one hand, the phone from the other. She licked her lips and took a few shallow breaths. "Let's go."

Claudia peered up the short stairway. Ascended with Zoey close behind. The landing outside the office was small, and solid. No exit there.

They skirted the office door. Claudia turned the knob, pushed the door open and it slammed against the wall.

Empty.

They searched, checking beneath the desk, behind the high-back chair, inside the rather large bathroom. No sign of the men, but no sign of an exit either.

Claudia tried the phone on the desk, checked the outlet for the connection. "Dammit. Phone's dead."

Zoey slumped in a leather chair. "This is nuts. Maybe we should bargain with James . . . "

"No, Zoey. There has to be an exit. There has to be a way in and out of this godforsaken place. We'll just have to start our search again. Maybe it's behind a hidden panel or something. Or in the vent system?" Claudia was searching the desk drawers.

Zoey got up and headed toward the bathroom. "I'll be right out." She'd put her injuries out of her mind until now, ignoring the pain, ignoring the wounds that reopened and spilled drops of blood every so often. Using the toilet wasn't going to be a pleasant experience. She winced against the inevitable pain and released her bladder. It hurt like hell but was somehow tolerable. A gentle, cool breeze refreshed her flushed skin.

Each room flashed in her mind, but she couldn't recall ever seeing anything that remotely resembled an exit. A hidden door, perhaps—there was bound to be one somewhere. But where?

Slumped against the back of the toilet seat, her heart now filled with renewed frustration. They'd come to far to be stopped this way. There had to be a way to get the information out of James.

She moistened a wad of toilet paper in the sink and tried to clean the blood and urine, winced against the febrile pain. Suddenly she looked up. *A cool breeze?* There was no air conditioning in the bathroom, no vents. She leaned against the sink and stood, walked toward the shower stall.

"I think I found something," Claudia said from the other side of the closed bathroom door. "On the desk, there was—"

It wasn't a shower after all. On the back wall, a door, obscured behind white tiles, the doorknob impossible to miss.

"Claudia! Come here!"

#

Using their same cautious approach, they opened the door and entered another office.

They searched it. A deep closet held dozens of outfits, including the clothes Zoey had been wearing the day she'd been kidnapped. She and Claudia quickly dressed. Zoey pulled on her too-large sweater and stroked the fabric, hugged herself, savoring the warmth and comfort. It smelled faintly of *Shalimar*, the fragrance she had been wearing that dreadful day. She climbed into her pants and they slid down her hips. Yanked them up and cinched them up with the cord from the dead phone. Slipped into her socks and boots and felt whole again.

The next room over was quarters for the guards, and they discovered identification, personal items; beds lined the walls military style.

They returned to the office. Several file cabinets housed hundreds of folders, each containing records and personal histories of the women downstairs, and presumably the women who had been here before them. Zoey's file was missing. Claudia searched for her own, but it, too, wasn't there.

Another door. They opened it, peered up a staircase dozens of steps high. Ascended, and once at the top discovered the door that James had described: solid oak, heavy, highly polished veneer. The keypad was near the knob.

"Fuck," Zoey muttered, leaning against the wall. "What do we do? Start punching numbers?"

Claudia grinned, and held up a note pad. "Let's start with these."

"What's that?"

"Maybe nothing, but I found it on the desk downstairs. There are several sets of numbers on here. Maybe James gave Sullivan the combination."

They punched the numbers at the bottom of the list into the keypad. Nothing. Several more attempts, and the lock clicked. Claudia turned the knob, and opened the door.

Zoey's stomach flip-flopped. Claudia peered out, gun raised. They entered yet another room, a small cabin. A tiny kitchenette in one corner, sofa near the fireplace. A deer head over the mantle sported a Yankees cap. The bathroom and closet were empty.

"This is their front," Claudia said, checking behind and beneath the sparse furniture. "A hunting cabin. Must have been their diversion."

The back of the oak door—the door to their personal Hell—was disguised to look like part of the paneling.

Outside, several cars were parked, covered in a layer of fresh snow. Patterns of fresh tire tracks indicated that several cars had recently taken off.

Claudia tried the cell phone. This time there was a signal. Dialed 9-1-1 and didn't know how to begin to explain.

Gun raised, Zoey checked the perimeter of the cabin, which looked deceptively ordinary from a distance. No indication of the atrocities inside.

The landscape left her awe-struck. Crystalline snow

embellished the trees like shards of glass, shining beneath the brilliance of a commanding moon. Zoey sobbed, lowered her gun, arms trembling. Breath plumed before her like clouds.

Claudia joined her. "They're on the way. I'm not sure they believed me at first."

Zoey nodded, unable to speak for the moment. Claudia wrapped her arms around Zoey's neck and hugged, sobbed into her shoulders.

"That's it," Zoey whispered, voice hitching, not wanting to let go. "This is finally over."

Claudia nodded against Zoey's neck. "Let's go tell everyone. I want to see the expression on James' face."

The line was left open, and the police traced the signal. Within an hour, the area was swarming with cops and paramedics.

Epilogue

A month had passed since the end of her ordeal, and Zoey was back in New York, trying to organize her life. Trying to make sense of it all.

December now, close to Christmas. When not in therapy, or visiting a myriad collection of doctors and specialists, she spent time at Rockefeller Center, gazing at the seventy-foot tree decorated with tens of thousands of tiny lights. Gave her comfort somehow; amid the crowds of Manhattan, she found peace and solitude. Felt safe surrounded by vast numbers, and felt safer still in open, unrestricted areas.

Her cell phone rang. Detective Ambrose, the one who had headed the investigation. "James was indicted today."

"I heard."

"Want to hear the list of charges?"

"Not really." Closed her eyes, leaned against the back of the bench, and wished James were out of her life once and for all, although she knew that would never happen. James and his staff of torturers were an indelible part of her past, and would be heady ghosts in her future. Kevin, however, was never arrested. Zoey had allowed him to escape.

A wet, frigid breeze whipped her cheeks. She pulled the corners of her jacket closer together.

"So far we've arrested two of the three men who fled. We have leads on the third, Zachary Williams. His associates are squealing like stuck pigs. We have reason to believe he's in Chicago."

"That's good news," she said.

There'd been a media circus when Zoey and the others had been rescued. Reporters dogged her around the clock, staking out her apartment, following her shopping or heading to appointments. A few of the other survivors gave interviews, and Jessica and Marie had even appeared on *Dateline*, but Zoey avoided it. Some were calling her a hero, a title she felt uncomfortable with.

"Paul, did they ever find my file? Did James mention what he'd done with it?"

James, it was revealed, was a filthy rich sociopath with little to do with his money. He'd been running his torture chamber for years, his employees either paid obscene amounts of money, or being blackmailed and threatened into compliance. Of the hundreds of women that had been kidnapped from up and down the eastern seaboard, and that he'd maintained files on, very few had ever resurfaced, dead or alive. Those few that did survive worked for him. Robin, Mel, and the woman who had called herself Dr. Chambers and introduced Zoey to the horrors in store through a quasi-medical exam.

The underground complex he'd built five years earlier was nestled in the Adirondack Mountains, on a tract of land he owned, thirty miles from the nearest highway or dirt road. Densely adorned with trees, rocks, wildflowers, the terrain didn't attract skiers. Didn't attract much of anyone, except for the occasional hiker.

"He told us he never touched your file, or Claudia's. There were four files missing, of all the women being held prisoner at the time."

"Four?" Ice skaters kept time with the organ music billowing from loudspeakers below the café. Dusk, Rockefeller Plaza. A light snow touched down, coating the city in a layer of baby powder.

"Yours, and Claudia, Jessica, and Marie."

James must have had something nasty in store for them, to have singled them out that way. She'd wondered why she'd been sent to the Nursery when her experience with the Visitors could have been so much less severe, especially since he had claimed to like her. He had to have moved the files before the Visitors took over, because he'd been beaten and restrained after the coup. The missing files belonged to the four women who had attacked, who had fought back, the four who had saved the others. It could have been that James knew who his real adversaries were. But why remove the files? For what purpose?

When she hung up with the detective she called Claudia, who was back home in Saratoga Springs, taking some time off before returning to the police force.

"Hi, it's Zoey. How are you holding up?"

Claudia sighed, cleared her throat. "You know how it goes. Hanging in there. How about you? Zoey, what did your doctor say?"

Her gynecologist had treated the extensive damage. It had taken two Xanax to get Zoey's feet in the stirrups. "Punctured colon, severe lacerations. She thinks my uterus isn't damaged. Not for the long term, anyway. They expect me to fully recover."

"That's wonderful news. My burns are healing, and my docs have given me a clean bill of health too. Hey—did you see my interview in *The News*?"

Zoey laughed. "I bought ten copies. You were wonderful! Listen, have you heard from Jess or Marie lately?"

"Not in a few days. Why?"

"Just wondering how they are." She was wondering about their missing files. "How's Tamara doing?"

Tamara, back in Baltimore. Recovering from her puncture wounds, palms and ankles torn and shredded, veins ruptured, severe tissue damage. Years' worth of recovery. "Still in the hospital, Zoey. Probably another month at least. Uh, Zoey . . . ?"

When Claudia didn't continue, Zoey whispered "Yes?"

There was another pause. " . . . Kim died this morning."

"Oh, no . . . " Zoey muttered, tears splashing her cheeks, falling to the ground when she bowed her head. God, not Kim. They'd been through so much together. "But her wound . . . " she said, choking on the words, trying to spit them out before it became impossible. "The gunshot wasn't that bad."

"I'm so sorry, Zoey. For all of us. Kim lost too much blood, and then the wound got infected. She also had severe internal damage."

"I'd better go," Zoey whispered, unable to stop the tears now. Before hanging up, she said to Claudia, "I want to thank you again for the care package. It was an incredible thing for you—"

But she couldn't finish the sentence. Had thanked Claudia before for the gift, had asked her if she'd get into trouble for sending Zoey something like that. Claudia had told her it was untraceable.

Doubled over she sobbed into her coat, trying to protect herself from curious stares from passers-by.

"My pleasure, hon," Zoey heard her say. "Please take care of yourself. And be careful."

"You, too," she squeaked, unable to say another word.

#

The subway home during the rush hour commute was packed. Just the way Zoey wanted it. She exited the N train station and headed toward her apartment a few blocks away.

The streets in her Queens neighborhood were relatively empty compared to Manhattan. The dusting of snow had chased everyone inside except for the smattering of children trying in vain to form snowballs from the loose powder.

Inside her apartment she turned on the TV. News reports of her ordeal were scarcer now compared to when the news broke but occasionally appeared, particularly when there was something newsworthy.

Such as James's indictment.

"Alleged ringleader of last month's Kidnap-Torture scandal, James Price was arraigned today, on charging including kidnapping, rape, and torture. He faces possible execution.

"As many as fifteen men and women have been charged in connection with the underground torture chamber, which was discovered in the Adirondack Mountains. Eighteen women were rescued, suffering from severe abuse. One woman, Kimberly Solomon, died earlier today from complications sustained during her ordeal."

James on the screen, sitting in court, his still-battered face looking solemn, his hands bandaged.

She lay on the bed on top of the blankets. Too early to call it a night, just resting her eyes. Impossible sometimes to relax. Images assaulted her desire to forget, to get on with her life. Her hand caressed the pillow, and she smiled when she remembered what was beneath it. Sleep had been fleeting but she was exhausted, and she dozed.

Pressure on her body woke her, and she panicked, believing for one horrible moment that the escape had been part of an elaborate dream, that she was still underground in the torture chamber.

She shook her head and blinked, tried to focus her eyes in a room lit only by the streetlight outside the bedroom window.

Zack was sitting on her stomach.

She threw her hands up to protect herself and to push him away. He punched her in the face.

"Fucking bitch," he snarled, hitting her again. "Do you *know* who you fucked with? Do you?" His hands wrapped around her neck. Tried to pry his fingers away, punched at his arms, kicked her legs up. Reached forward until her fingers found his face and dug them into his eyes.

He yelled, released her, clutched his wound. "You cunt!"

She knocked him off and scrambled away, but he caught her leg.

She looked up, caught the glint of metal just before he plunged it into her side. The pain was excruciating, filled her body with razored claws of heat.

He pulled out the knife. She dragged herself toward the pillow. Felt the knife stab her thigh. Screamed in agony.

"Die, you fucking bitch!" He tried to pull her toward him but she kicked free. He struck again but missed, tearing open the mattress instead.

Finally reached the pillow, groped beneath it, wrapped her fingers around Claudia's gift.

He flipped her on her back, straddled her, and with the knife in both hands he raised his arms overhead. Just as he drove it into her stomach she pulled the trigger, blowing away most of Zack's stunned expression.

Blood bubbled out of her mouth, gushed from gashes on her body. Sobbed, reached for the phone. So weak . . . barely able to reach it. Picked up the receiver and listened. No dial tone.

"God . . . " she groaned, vomiting blood. Fell to her hands and knees on the floor, crawled toward the living room. Cell phone, on the coffee table. Thick gore trailed her across the room.

She'd gotten him. Knew she'd probably saved Jess, Claudia and Marie from the maniac. Knew they would have been next. She smiled, suddenly feeling no pain, feeling instead a comfortable warmth, like being immersed in a soothing bath.

Punched 9-1-1 on the cell phone keypad. " . . . Need . . . help . . . " she muttered, leaning against the sofa, life's blood escaping through fingers pressed against her stomach.

Couldn't talk anymore, even when the dispatcher asked her questions. "Don't hang up the phone. Help is on the way. Can you hear me?"

Zoey dropped the phone. Closed her eyes, the hint of a smile on her lips.

She was finally free.

Lightning Source UK Ltd.
Milton Keynes UK
UKOW041946241012

201149UK00001B/55/A